The Saint's Magic Power is Omnipotent

Oscar

A merchant entrusted with Sei's company. At least, that's how he was introduced. However, he's actually...

Jude

A researcher at the Research Institute of Medicinal Flora. Also traveling with Sei.

Ceyran

The captain of a trading vessel from abroad. What will Sei do when she sees what he has to offer?

Sei

The Saint who was summoned to another world. In disguise, since she's traveling incognito.

I turned my face to him. He smiled sweetly at me.

His passionate gaze scored a direct hit. I missed a step, but Albert quickly righted me.

This is taking all I've got. Please don't attack me like that right now!

"Sei. Look at me?"

Table of Contents

The Saint's Magic Power is Omnipotent

WRITTEN BY
Yuka Tachibana

ILLUSTRATED BY
Yasuyuki Syuri

Seven Seas Entertainment

The head researcher at the Research Institute of Medicinal Flora. Keeps an eye on and takes care of Sei. Friends with Albert since childhood.

Grand magus of the Royal Magi Assembly. His only interest is in research related to magic and magical powers. Has taken a keen interest in Sei.

A researcher at the Research Institute of Medicinal Flora and in charge of teaching Sei. Caring and friendly. Frequently comes to snitch the food Sei makes.

Aira Misono, a high schooler who was summoned to another world like Sei. Studying magic at the Royal Magi Assembly.

The daughter of a marquis whom Sei befriended at the library. Looks up to Sei.

Magus of the Royal Magi Assembly and Albert's older brother. A man of few words who has common sense. Always being manipulated by Yuri.

Characters

The Saint's Magic Power is Omnipotent

Sei

Sei Takanashi, an office lady who was summoned to another world to be the Saint. She's been healing people and purging monsters, and recently has been troubled by the fact that all over the place, people have begun to worship her. Enjoys cooking and making cosmetics.

Leonhardt

The leader of the mercenary company in Klausner's Domain. He takes a liking to Sei for her great skill as an alchemist.

Albert Hawke

Knight commander of the Knights of the Third Order. Known as the "Ice Knight" for his supposedly frigid demeanor, but toward Sei, he's...?

The moment she got home from working overtime at the office, Sei Takanashi, an office lady in her twenties, was abruptly summoned to another world. Although Sei was summoned to be the Saint, the crown prince of the kingdom exited the room with only Aira Misono, the cute high school girl who had been summoned with Sei, leaving Sei behind.

Sei had no notion of how to return to Japan, so she soon decided to begin working at the palace's Research Institute of Medicinal Flora.

Although Sei realized that she was indeed the Saint, she concealed the truth in order to live her life as an ordinary person. However, Sei displayed tremendous magical ability, astounding everyone with her skills in potion-making, cooking, and concocting cosmetics.

Starting from the day she used one of her high-grade HP potions to save Knight Commander Albert Hawke's life, Sei performed one miracle after another. In time, rumor in the palace began to suggest that Sei Takanashi was the true Saint.

Although she was summoned by the Royal Magi Assembly to be the Saint, Sei managed to avoid being outed for some time. She took up intensive magical training under the guidance of Grand Magus Yuri Drewes, and her days were busy yet fulfilling.

Perhaps as a result of her training, or perhaps by mere coincidence, Sei performed another miracle with her gold-colored magic, strengthening suspicions that she was the Saint. However, Crown Prince Kyle denounced those suspicions, stubbornly upholding Aira as the true Saint.

However, on a monster-slaying expedition, Sei once and for all proved her Sainthood. When Knight Commander Albert Hawke was in danger, Sei called on her golden magic to instantly cleanse the black miasma producing the monsters.

As a result, Crown Prince Kyle was confined to his quarters for accusing Sei of being a false Saint. Furthermore, Aira, who had been isolated by Kyle once she arrived in the kingdom, was finally able to make friends at the academy, and with Sei. She, too, now strives for a peaceful life.

Due to the miraculous power of her golden magic, Sei was finally recognized as the true Saint. However, she still couldn't figure out how exactly to consistently call on her Saintly power.

Even so, Sei received a request to visit Klausner's Domain—the alchemist's holy land. She enjoyed the trip at first, where she became the apprentice of a master alchemist, befriended the captain of a mercenary company, and explored the possibilities of medicinal cooking.

Then, while working with her new teacher, Sei came across the memoirs of a previous Saint. Thanks to a hint in the memoirs, Sei finally figured out how to use the Saint's special powers—but the key to calling on them was so embarrassing that she couldn't tell anyone. She had to think about Knight Commander Hawke!

However, now that Sei could use the Saint's power, she could do what she had come to do: go into the forest with the knights and mercenaries, and slay the monsters within.

Now able to use the Saint's power at will, Sei headed into the forests of Klausner's Domain, where valuable herbs grew in abundance. Though she was protected by the knights and mercenaries, as they proceeded into the forest depths, they encountered slimes—monsters resistant to physical attacks!

They were soon surrounded. After a grueling fight, Sei and her companions managed to escape back to the castle. There, they discussed how to reach the forest's heart, as they lacked the magical firepower to defeat the slimes. Luckily, Grand Magus Yuri Drewes arrived, Aira in tow.

With the help of these powerful reinforcements, Sei successfully purified the forest and brought peace to Klausner's Domain. However, one thing still troubled Sei: the tragic state of the forest devastated by the slimes. In secret, Sei used the power of the Saint to miraculously revive the forest.

During the victory banquet, Sei and Aira helped with the cooking and grew closer with the mercenaries. However, with her Saintly mission now completed, it was time to leave. Though it pained Sei and company to say farewell to their new companions, they couldn't help feeling cheerful as they made their way back to the capital.

SEIJO NO MARYOKU WA BANNO DESU VOL. 5

First published in Japan in 2020 by
KADOKAWA CORPORATION, Tokyo.
English translation rights arranged with
KADOKAWA CORPORATION, Tokyo.

Seven Seas press and purchase enquiries can be sent to Marketing Manager Lianne Sentar at press@gomanga.com. Information regarding the distribution and purchase of digital editions is available from Digital Manager CK Russell at digital@gomanga.com.

Follow Seven Seas Entertainment online at
sevenseasentertainment.com.

TRANSLATION: Julie Goniwich
COVER DESIGN: Nicky Lim
LOGO DESIGN: George Panella
INTERIOR LAYOUT & DESIGN: Clay Gardner
COPY EDITOR: Jade Gardner
PROOFREADER: Rebecca Schneidereit
LIGHT NOVEL EDITOR: E.M. Candon
PREPRESS TECHNICIAN: Melanie Ujimori
PRINT MANAGER: Rhiannon Rasmussen-Silverstein
PRODUCTION MANAGER: Lissa Pattillo
MANAGING EDITOR: Julie Davis
ASSOCIATE PUBLISHER: Adam Arnold
PUBLISHER: Jason DeAngelis

ISBN: 978-1-64827-363-6
Printed in Canada
First Printing: January 2022
10 9 8 7 6 5 4 3 2 1

Trading Company

THREE MONTHS HAD PASSED since my return to the capital following my adventures in Klausner's Domain. The days were growing warmer, and summer was nearly upon us. It would be my second summer in this new world.

Since my return, I had been kept busy heading out to different domains at the palace's request, where I helped rid the kingdom of ever more monsters. The work was nonstop, but purging one black swamp after another left me feeling fulfilled—like I was doing something truly good for the world. Everywhere we visited saw a clear decrease in the local monster population, and that brought me peace of mind for the time being.

However, we hadn't yet been able to determine whether the overall monster population had actually fallen. It was entirely possible that for every black swamp I purified, another popped up somewhere else. Thus, the search for the black swamps continued, and whenever another one was found, we headed out to take care of it.

If a domain didn't have a black swamp, its troubles were typically left up to the knights to deal with; I didn't go with them in these cases. As a result, I'd had a bit of free time on my hands of late. And, as it happened, a sizable delivery from Klausner's Domain had just arrived at the Research Institute of Medicinal Flora.

"This is incredible," I murmured as I took in the pyramid of boxes in the storeroom.

The mountain-high stack of boxes contained seeds and herbs from Klausner's Domain—and not just the herbs we needed to make standard potions, of which we presently had a shortage. They'd also sent ingredients for potions that cured abnormal status effects like burns and paralysis. My colleagues shouted for joy as they perused the contents of the delivery and scanned the attached inventory. Perhaps it would be more accurate to say that they *roared* with joy. Apparently, we had received some incredibly rare plants.

Wow, that guy's normally so quiet. It must be a big deal if he's being so loud! As I observed my coworker's curious behavior, Johan, the head researcher of the institute, came over with a letter in hand.

"Sei, a letter for you came with the shipment."

It had been privately addressed to me and been brought to the institute with the rest. I turned it over to find Corinna's name on it. I opened the envelope on the spot to read. I couldn't help but chuckle dryly to myself. She had found out about my last little adventure before I left Klausner's Domain, when I had revived the forest ravaged by the slimes. She had also guessed that I wanted this to be a secret; she didn't explicitly state what she knew, but the letter was written in such a way that anyone who knew what she was referring to would immediately recognize what she meant. She ended the missive with a most courteous thank you.

I suspected that the lavish gifts in this shipment meant that Corinna had informed Lord Klausner of my actions. The fact that I, who knew jack squat about politics, had figured out as much really spoke to just how many plants we had received from Klausner's Domain...especially as a few more things arrived, which had been addressed to "Sei at the Institute."

You read correctly. They sent additional gifts to me, specifically, although these were in a different storeroom. The herb shortage wasn't yet over, so Corinna and Lord Klausner must have gone out of their way to scrape together what they could just for me. I felt a bit bad about it, but I was touched by Corinna's thoughtfulness. It really warmed my heart.

Johan had been busily checking the boxes with the other researchers, but he noticed I was done reading the letter and came back over to me.

"What was it about?" he asked with a grin, but he was more focused on the bag in his hand. I assumed it contained seeds, given that the name of a well-known plant rarely found on the market was written on the bag. Johan was so pleased he was practically grinning ear to ear.

"It was a thank-you letter for killing the monsters. And the herbs seem to be gifts of gratitude."

"I see. You went and did something crazy again, didn't you?" he teased.

I pouted slightly. "What a rude thing to say. I did no such thing." I paused, feeling slightly guilty. "I think?"

That was probably a mistake. Johan's tone was immediately exasperated. "The way you make that sound like a question makes me all the more suspicious."

I looked in a completely different direction and heard him sigh deeply.

"Although, I did hear some of what happened out there from Al," Johan added with a faint smile.

I broke out in a cold sweat. "D-did you now?"

Had he heard about what I had done in the slime forest?

From his tone, that didn't seem too likely. I had a feeling that if he had, he wouldn't be merely exasperated—I'd be facing down a full-fledged scolding. Johan had to tell me to restrain myself basically every day of the year, so all I could do was pray that he never discovered how far I'd gone to save the forest.

I swiftly changed the subject back to our glorious haul. "At any rate, with all this, we'll be able to move right ahead with our research too."

Johan responded just as I anticipated. "Indeed. We'll even be able to pick up the projects we had to put on pause due to the herb shortage. Speaking of, I couldn't help but notice that among the seeds addressed to you, there were some for herbs that we can't grow locally."

"I bet they're the ones I asked for."

"Is that so?"

"I learned a new cultivation technique while I was in Klausner's Domain, so I wanted to try growing them here too."

"Oho."

"I might want your help with it."

"I wouldn't mind that at all."

As Johan's research focused on cultivating herbs, he was much more interested in the seeds than the end product. I was impressed by the volume of knowledge he brought to bear after only glimpsing the herb's name on the bag.

I wanted to try all sorts of things with both seeds that required blessed soil in order to grow and seeds that didn't. Between my Saint's magic and Johan's Earth Magic, I wondered if we might be able to grow anything we put our minds to, no matter the climate and soil a plant usually required.

As Johan had agreed to help so easily, I decided that I would reward him by cooking a new dish later.

Moreover, we really had been sent a *ton* of herbs. Surely it would be okay for me to use some of them for things other than potions. Some of the samples sent specifically for me included herbs that could be used in cosmetics. Maybe I could try making a new type of moisturizer or cream. I loved how the scent of a product changed based on which herbs you used.

I'd also been tanning a bit, due to all the expeditions lately, so I figured it would be a good idea to make something that would protect me from the effects of the sun.

"What's on your mind?" Johan asked.

I had gone quiet as I watched the researchers still frolicking about the boxes. "Nothing. I was just thinking about trying to make some new creams with my share of the shipment."

"Oh?" Johan sounded suspicious, and he eyed me with equal skepticism. When I defended myself—I was just thinking about different fragrances and effects that I might be able to experiment with versus the kinds I'd already used—he nodded. "Well, then. So, you want to make even more new health and beauty products..."

"Is something wrong?"

"Oh, no, just...are you planning to sell those to that company in the city as well?"

"I hadn't thought about that in particular, no."

"I see. Well, I bet a number of people would want to buy them."

"Ah... You're probably right."

Oof, I'd kind of forgotten about that. The cosmetics I made were in high demand, seeing as the ones I made were extremely effective. Apparently, my Pharmaceuticals skill really shone when it came to beauty care.

I had originally made a handful of cosmetics for my own personal use, but upon witnessing their effects for herself, Liz had asked me to make some for her as well, which was how I'd started sharing them. The effects had been evident in Liz's case as well, at which point her friends had started gossiping about her new cosmetics, which had in turn led to a ton of people begging her to share her source.

It had been one thing to make cosmetics exclusively for Liz, but no way could I have made enough for all those people. I had my work at the institute too, after all. So, I had asked Johan for assistance, and we had sold my recipe to a certain trading company, which now made the cosmetics for me.

Admittedly, things had grown a bit intense after I told Liz that this company would start carrying my cosmetics. Even more people than expected had flocked to the store to buy them. Johan told me that while the company was used to dealing with products in high demand, they'd had a hard time managing the daily queue of nobles lined up outside their store.

These days, the company had a system by which it was able to fulfill regular orders for all its customers. However, things could well get hectic if a new product suddenly debuted. It wasn't hard to imagine a repeat of the initial buying frenzy. It would be best to carefully consider all angles before introducing a new product into the market.

"We should probably talk to someone from the company about it," I agreed.

"My thoughts exactly. I'll go ahead and get in touch with them."

"Great!"

I had nothing to worry about when I left Johan in charge.

I went back to mulling over what to make as I returned to the inventory of herbs that had been sent to me. Because I was so absorbed in my own thoughts, I didn't notice Johan's thoughtful expression as he left the storehouse.

◆◆◆

On days when I had to attend my multitude of classes on etiquette, I had to brace myself for transforming into a noble lady. Yet again, I found myself in a room in the royal palace at the crack of dawn, surrounded by maids. Mary, the attendant in charge of my personal maids, noticed a bottle on top of the dresser, one she had never seen before.

"Lady Sei, do you know what this is?" she asked as she cradled the white porcelain bottle in her hands.

"Oh, that's a new skincare cream."

As soon as I said that, the other maids zeroed in on me. Their gazes were so intense that they were almost audible.

"What does it do?"

"It should protect your skin from sun damage—or even reverse it."

"Reverse the effects of the sun..." the maid next to me murmured.

Somewhere, someone gulped.

I couldn't be too surprised by this reaction. Fair skin was a big part of the Kingdom of Salutania's classic beauty standards. That was why noble ladies always took care not to let themselves tan. However, sometimes sun exposure was unavoidable, which was especially troublesome for the maids who worked at the palace. After all, the maids were also noble ladies, and with all their obligations, they had to work incredibly hard to avoid getting an uneven skin tone. As such, they were keenly interested in anything that might protect their skin. I totally understood.

"Is this cream a finished product?" one maid asked tentatively.

"I'm testing it on myself first. Once I've determined that it's safe, I'd love it if you all tested it for me as well."

The maid's expression changed to one of joy, and she nodded eagerly. "We would be more than happy to assist!"

Normally, Mary would have chided her, but this time she merely chuckled. I suspected that she was interested in this brand-new cream too.

I needed to test it to ensure I hadn't accidentally included any common allergens or anything—I didn't want customers getting rashes after the company started selling it. Therefore, I was the first guinea pig, and if that went well, I'd ask others to try it as well.

The last time I had a new product—or rather, the first time—I'd had my maids test it as well. They had been more than happy to help me out, since it meant they got to test the hot new beauty products the other noble ladies were all raving about. The results of the last round had been uniformly excellent, which is to say, the maids had been overjoyed by their outcomes. As such, they'd begged me to let them help the next time I concocted a new product. I'd been hoping they were still interested, and I was glad that they seemed eager to dive right back into testing.

"So it won't just prevent damage, it'll repair your skin, correct?"

"I can't wait to see how much it'll even out my skin tone!"

My maids chattered excitedly as they brought over my dress and accessories. Their eyes practically sparkled in anticipation.

"Don't get your hopes up—it might not be as effective as you want. It really depends on the person." I laughed nervously, trying to temper their expectations, but it didn't really work.

"Not a soul in the palace doubts the effectiveness of your creations, Lady Sei."

"So true. I *only* use your cosmetics now."

Perhaps the results wouldn't be as amazing as they hoped, but there would definitely be *some* kind of effect. My new cream was made with several herbs said to be good for your skin, so I expected it to have a number of desirable effects.

For example, my skin had grown a bit red due to working in the institute's gardens, and whenever I used the cream myself, the redness instantly vanished. It disappeared so quickly that I was wondering whether the cream could more accurately be called a topical potion.

However, I didn't know if the cream would lighten tans as suddenly as it had healed my burns. My skin was usually as pale as it could naturally be due to all the time I spent cooped up in the institute, so it was hard for me to tell how well it worked on that front. I feared the effects would be similarly minimal even for my future customers, so I was a bit worried that I'd fail to meet expectations this time around.

The maids dismissed my worrying. If anything, they were more cheerful than usual. They still managed to work swiftly to get me ready, just as they always did.

The next morning, Johan called me to a meeting. He also asked me to bring tea, so I stopped at the dining hall to make some before heading to his office. He asked for four cups. One had to be for Johan, but who were the other three for?

Did we have guests coming today? I wondered as I knocked on the door. "Please excuse the interruption."

"Sorry to bother you so early in the morning."

Inside the room, I saw not one but two people I didn't recognize. Who were these guys?

Johan encouraged me to sit down next to him. "Allow me to introduce you to Franz and Oscar."

"How do you do? My name is Franz," said one.

"And mine is Oscar," said the other. "It's nice to meet you."

"It's nice to meet you both as well. I'm Sei."

Across from me were seated two gentlemen. The older one, Franz, had white hair and dark blue eyes the color of sapphires. The younger one beside him, Oscar, had orange hair and bright green eyes the color of emeralds.

Franz was thin, and his white hair was swept back neatly. He also wore glasses. Unlike Lord Smarty-Glasses, though, he wore a genial smile on his face and looked like the very image of a good-natured old man. For some reason, he carried himself with really capable anime butler vibes. I almost wanted to call him "Sebastian" in my mind.

Oscar, on the other hand, had a medium build with hair that pointed out a bit here and there. His catlike eyes had a lively look, which gave him an animated appearance. He looked to be about Jude's age—or maybe a little older? Younger than Johan, at least.

They didn't appear to be nobles, given their clothes, but they did seem wealthy, somehow. My impression was pretty much on the mark. Johan explained that these two were from a trading company. Franz was actually the chairman, and Oscar was his assistant.

"You're merchants, then?" I asked.

"Indeed, they are. I was thinking of starting a new business venture," Johan said.

"Oh, really?"

"Yes, yours."

"Huh?"

I gave Johan a questioning look, so he went on in more detail. Up until now, we had been selling the cosmetics I devised through Franz's company. However, due to the products' popularity, they were making an almost egregious amount of money. Consequently, they had earned the ire of competing companies, and a number of problems had arisen.

Johan had originally chosen to work with a company affiliated with his family, House Valdec, as that made it easier for him to oversee the company's many moving parts versus just getting a profit report. However, with all the new tensions cropping up, Johan kept having to get more involved, and it was becoming difficult to juggle both the business and his work at the institute. Recently, another noble family had even started moving in on the company, so Johan's family members were also getting looped into dealing with it.

I was incredibly grateful to Johan for going to such lengths for my benefit, seeing as I knew nothing at all about business. Thanks to the arrangements he'd made, I got a return on the profits and had increased my personal assets. I felt incredibly guilty when I heard that his whole family was being affected by these events.

And here I was, considering selling a whole new product. This new Get Rich Quick (Again) scheme would definitely stir up even more tensions. Therefore, Johan had decided to cut ties with the company Franz represented. Instead, from now on, we would sell all the products I developed through a new company that had nothing to do with House Valdec. That way we could minimize the impact on Johan's life.

But would the problems really just poof into thin air because a different company was selling my cosmetics? Johan insisted that they would.

"Who would be foolhardy enough to challenge the Saint's company?"

I frowned, still feeling dubious. "Well, I guess you're right."

However, the merchants nodded and backed up Johan's assessment.

I guess it's only natural considering the Saint's position in Salutanian society... I still wasn't convinced, but I set those doubts aside for the time being. If this was going to be *my* company, then I had other questions I wanted answered.

"Why should the company be mine, though? I'm only good at developing stuff," I said, trying to articulate my anxieties. The only things I could do for a business would be to make potions or other pharmaceutical-adjacent products. I didn't know the first thing about running a business.

"I'm aware. That's why I called these two." Johan nodded to the merchants.

The plan was that I could just do what I had always done and brew whatever new thing I thought of while Franz and Oscar here would take care of everything else regarding the company. Therefore, the only real difference from how we'd done it before would be who I went to when I'd come up with something new—I would still be doing the same things and would receive the same compensation as before.

Franz and Oscar had been hand-selected from the original company and were highly skilled in their areas. I really could just leave everything to them. I worried that their prior employers would sorely miss such capable people, but Johan assured me that his family was helping the company adjust as needed.

I was beginning to suspect I owed House Valdec a hefty thank-you gift.

"We look forward to working with you," said Franz, smiling serenely while Oscar grinned with a bow.

Well, Johan had given them his stamp of approval, so I was sure my work would be safe in their qualified hands.

"I look forward to working with you as well," I said.

With that, our introductions were complete.

◆ ◆ ◆

One month after I was introduced to Franz and Oscar, a new shop opened in the royal capital, run by a new company of which Franz was chairman. It was located on a street lined with other stores that served noble clientele. Franz had chosen this location since, in short, the nobility were the primary customer base he intended to court.

However, the shop was also close to a street that prioritized serving commoners. Franz had anticipated that, soon enough, wealthy commoners would wish to become customers of our shop as well. He had been right on the money.

I observed the shop from a little ways away. It was filled with not only nobles but young ladies who looked to be from merchant families. The ladies had all brought their servants as well, so the shop was profoundly crowded.

I bet it's not that unusual for a shop on a street corner in a luxury goods district to be so bustling, I thought as I watched. "Business sure is booming."

"Quite. It looks like your cosmetics are even more popular than we anticipated," Oscar agreed.

"Yeah. You know, only the nobility bought them at the old store."

"I hear they turned quite a profit too—every merchant in the capital knew of their success. The noblewomen couldn't stop talking about it."

"Was the old store noble-exclusive, then?"

"Yup. Mostly because they couldn't keep up with demand. Franz really is grateful that we were able to re-expand our customer base, thanks to your suggestion."

Oscar and I had spent a lot of time talking to one another this past month while getting the shop up and running, so we were now on casual speaking terms. At first, he had been exceedingly polite, but he had just been conducting himself as he thought he ought to. I much preferred being informal with people, though, so the second he eased up, I'd let him dip into more laid-back speech without telling him off for it.

However, I was pretty much the only one who felt that way. The person standing on the opposite side of me side-eyed Oscar something awful. This person was none other than Knight Commander Albert Hawke, who was with us as my escort in the city.

Actually, Albert was acting a bit different than usual; his face was oddly expressionless as he watched Oscar with a keen eye. "What did you suggest?" he finally asked, his interest apparently piqued by Oscar's words.

I wasn't sure if Oscar had noticed the look Albert was giving him, but he responded in a far more formal tone of voice. "Lady Sei proposed an excellent solution—on her advice, we divided our product lines based on relative effectiveness."

In other words, I had suggested to Franz that we sell cheaper products as well. Before, we had employed individuals who possessed the Pharmaceuticals skill to make our products, so they had cost a bit more. However, as the recipes I used had originated in my old world, they could be made by people who didn't possess any such relevant skills. Granted, the products were much less effective when brewed by someone without said skills. All the same, I figured we could sell them too—but at a lower price.

We could now see the result of that diversification. The shop made clear that the new line was less effective than the original one, but a huge number of people still wanted to buy the new products.

"Is everything else going well?" I asked Oscar.

"Very much so." Oscar grinned. "The new hires are uniformly excellent. I expect things should continue to go swimmingly."

"That's great to hear."

"Will you be stopping by again soon?"

"I'd like to. It's just a bit crowded today."

"Got it. Then will you be heading straight home?"

"That was the plan."

"Well, you came all this way into the capital, so why not stop by somewhere on your way? There's a popular café that recently opened."

"Is that so?"

"Mm-hmm. It caters to nobility, but I hear they've got unusual blends of imported tea. All the nobles who like trying new things are raving about the place these days."

Tea from another country? The thought piqued my interest quite a bit. However, if I went, that meant Albert would have to join me, as he was my escort.

I came here for leisure, but Albert's still on the clock. Can I really ask him to accompany me somewhere just for fun? Probably not, huh? For some reason, I felt guilty just thinking about it. I already felt like I'd added to his workload because I'd wanted to see how the shop was doing. I really wanted to check out that café, but I really, *really* didn't want to bother him.

I was just about to politely decline Oscar's suggestion when Albert spoke. "Where's this café?"

Oscar rattled off the directions as I stared.

Huh? Why? I haven't even said anything yet. Is Albert interested in going too? I blinked at Albert as he listened to Oscar's directions. Albert noticed my gaze, and our eyes met.

"You want to go, don't you?" he asked.

"Huh? Well, yes."

"Then let's go sample their tea."

Really? He smiled so sweetly as he said it—it made me suddenly all the more desperate to go. Had he seen through my hesitation? Or had it been blindingly obvious that I wanted to go?

After we left Oscar and headed off to the café, I broke down and asked how he'd figured me out.

"Your eyes," he said. "They sparkled the second he mentioned the café. It was more or less the same look you have whenever the topic turns to herbs and potions."

Did I really get some kind of *look* on my face when I talked about those things? More importantly, did I really think herbs and potions were as exciting as a new café?! I dropped my gaze to my feet, feeling just a wee bit mortified. I heard muffled laughter at my side. I couldn't help but glare at Albert with narrowed eyes.

After a few minutes of rocking in the carriage, we arrived at the café.

"This must be the place."

"Whoa!"

The café sported an enormous glass window that looked out onto the road, so we were able to see its interior from the outside. Maybe because it was a café that served only noble clientele, it wasn't too crowded. It did still have some other customers, though.

Albert escorted me in. The waiter welcomed us with a smile and led us farther inside. A painted landscape covered the wall on the right, while on the left, a series of mirrors helped make the café appear larger than it was.

Well, if this place serves nobles, I guess they have to go all out with the interior decorating, I thought as I sat at the table we were brought to.

Without looking at the menu, I told the waiter that we wanted a drink that had been imported. He smiled and nodded as if he knew exactly what I was asking for. It was only after he walked away that I realized I should have asked for a bite to eat as well. Too late now, though. I'd just been too curious about this brand-new type of tea I had never tried before!

Soon enough, the waiter returned and presented our drinks.

"This is coffee, our establishment's signature beverage."

I gasped in surprise. *Coffee?! He did just say coffee, right?!*

I gazed fixedly at the offered cup. The swaying black liquid made my heart soar beyond my wildest dreams. I never could have expected it would actually be the real deal.

For reasons I still didn't know, when I had been summoned, the words from this world had automatically been replaced with Japanese (or other languages from my old world). However, the translation process sometimes influenced my impression of things in an unexpected way. Pretty much the only things I had drunk since coming to this world had been water or tea—definitely not coffee. Had my brain replaced the word Oscar used to describe this beverage with "tea"? Or maybe it was just that Oscar thought that coffee was a type of tea and he really had said "tea."

Wait, that wasn't the point! I couldn't believe that they were actually serving *coffee*.

"What is it?" Albert asked worriedly.

I was still frozen, staring silently at the cup. "Oh, I was just surprised. I recognize this drink."

His expression grew even more anxious. "Do you know it from your home country?"

"Yeah." I smiled. *All's well,* I assured him with my eyes. His expression softened.

It had been so, so, *so* long since I last had coffee. It would have been a waste not to drink it while it was still hot. I picked up the cup and brought it to my lips. The nostalgic scent tickled my nose, and my smile deepened all on its own.

I had drunk coffee every day, back in Japan.

"It has a far stronger flavor than tea," said Albert.

"Yeah. And I bet it'll taste wonderful with milk."

The coffee the café brewed was much stronger than what I was used to. I tipped the cup, and at the bottom, I found coffee grounds. This drink was probably closer to Turkish coffee than anything.

"Hmm? I thought this wasn't your first time drinking this."

"I've had coffee before, but this tastes different from the kind we have back in Japan. I think it's probably because they're brewing it differently."

"Does that matter?"

"Yes, it can make quite a difference in flavor."

Back in Japan, I had enjoyed a lot of canned and drip coffee. There were scads of other ways to brew it, such as nel drip, vacuum coffee makers, or French press, but I had never tried coffee brewed using those methods before—to say nothing of Turkish coffee.

"Did you drink it a lot back in Japan?"

"I used to drink it every day! It makes you feel less sleepy."

I'd read that the feeling of being more awake after drinking coffee was more a placebo effect than anything. Regardless, I had habitually enjoyed a can or a cup after lunch. I always ended up a bit nauseated if I had more than two cups though, so it wasn't like I slugged them down one after another. I still hadn't been able to stop myself from having coffee once after breakfast and again after lunch.

"Really?" Albert asked.

"I used to even make it myself."

"You did?"

"Mm-hmm. With the right tools, I bet I could do it here too."

When I thought about the tools at my disposal, I imagined a beaker and a flask from the institute would probably do the trick, even if I didn't know how exactly

I'd use them. Although, if I figured out how to do the nel drip technique—which involved filtering hot water through coffee grounds held in a cloth—I might be able to make it work with just a cloth and a wire.

"Did you think of something?" Albert asked.

"Yeah. I think I might be able to pull together what I'd need to make Japanese-style coffee."

"Really?"

If I got all the equipment I needed, there was just one more thing I needed to do.

Even though I didn't say anything, Albert's eyes lit up in anticipation of what would come next. Of course I would treat him to my own special brew! Assuming I actually managed to make it.

The real question: Did they sell coffee beans at the café? I wouldn't be able to even attempt making my own coffee if they didn't. I flagged down the waiter to ask him, and I was in luck. Apparently, other customers had also expressed a desire to make their own coffee.

In the end, we bought a small bag of coffee beans before we headed back to the palace. Notably, as one might expect for an imported product, the beans did wind up costing a pretty penny indeed.

The Saint's Magic Power is Omnipotent

Act 2
Imported Products

"YOU'RE DRINKING IT again?"

The moment I entered Johan's office to deliver some documents, the smell of coffee hit my nose. If memory served, every time I'd come into his office since that fateful day in the capital, the room had brimmed with that telltale fragrance. He was becoming a bit of an addict, that Johan was.

"Don't say it like that," he protested. "I'll have you know I bought these beans with my own personal funds."

"I know, I know. But it's just not healthy to drink too much of it! You've been going at it nonstop recently, haven't you?"

Johan averted his gaze. I couldn't help but chuckle.

However, I wasn't really one to talk—it was my fault that coffee had gained such popularity at the institute in the first place.

Immediately after I got back to the institute on the day that I had coffee with Albert, I went and asked Johan if he knew someone who could make the brewing apparatuses I described. He did. He'd had no idea what he was in for, or so the saying went.

Johan referred me to the artisans who produced the experiment apparatuses for the institute. We summoned someone from the workshop to visit the institute, and I explained what I wanted made. It had been delivered a week later looking just as I had described it.

Once I had both coffee beans and the proper tools, I went ahead and brewed coffee in the institute's dining hall. As this drink was the latest fad in the capital, a number of people gathered to watch, their interest piqued. Johan had been first in line. All eyes were on me as I used my brand-new nel drip to slowly brew the coffee.

Murmurs of interest and admiration spread through the hall as the spectators watched the black liquid drip through the filter into the glass pot. While some of my colleagues didn't care for the unfamiliar smell, the majority of them found it tantalizing. What else could you expect from researchers at an institute that specialized in medicinal flora? They were so used to the smell of herbs that a number of them easily tolerated a strange new fragrance.

Many of them wanted to taste it right away as well. Although some of them had already tried coffee at that café. Those who had, ended up concluding that the coffee I made was easier to drink. I had to assume that was because the taste of nel drip coffee wasn't nearly as strong as that of Turkish coffee.

Long story short, coffee was now all the rage at the institute.

"Please only drink it in moderation," I urged Johan. "We had a word for caffeine intoxication back in Japan, you know—caffeinism. It's not good for your health to drink too much of the stuff."

"Fine, fine. I'll watch my intake. But you don't imagine I have enough to actually grow intoxicated, do you?" He chuckled dryly.

"I suppose."

He wasn't wrong. Coffee beans were imported from abroad, so they were quite expensive. As a result, Johan took his coffee in a small cup, meaning he never drank that much at once. No matter how many of those itty bitty cups he drank in one day, he'd be hard-pressed to reach the point of intoxication.

Nevertheless, I couldn't help but worry. The coffee in this world was much stronger than the coffee I remembered in Japan.

Coffee had become popular at the institute for more than its taste. While its anti-drowsiness effects had been up for debate in Japan, it was quite apparent that coffee really worked here. I was shocked to see that by drinking coffee, a person who had worked through the night for three days straight could still manage to be bright-eyed and mentally on the ball. One of my colleagues had even proposed that we might be able to call coffee a potion that cured abnormal status effects—specifically those that caused a person to sleep.

Consequently, the dangers of coffee were on my mind. My colleagues were a little too overjoyed at the thought of being able to cut down on how much they needed to sleep. I had never heard anyone warn against drinking too many potions, but I was starting to worry that people were drinking too much coffee to their detriment.

Fortunately, the cups Johan drank were usually made by the chefs, so at least there was that. The person who'd stayed awake for three days straight had done so after he drank one of my brews. My fifty-percent-bonus curse was at it again, though I wasn't sure if the culprit this time had been my Pharmaceuticals skill or my Cooking skill.

After handing Johan the documents, I headed back to my station and bumped into Jude in the hallway. He was on his way back from fetching some herbs from the storehouse. We acknowledged one another and continued to the workroom together. As we walked, I asked Jude about something I had thought of just the other day.

Having run across coffee, I had started longing for the flavors of my home country. Since Jude came from a family of merchants that specialized in food, I wanted to ask him about something. He seemed likely to know about the plants they dealt in.

"Rice?" he asked. "That's a new one for me."

"You've never even heard of such a grain?"

"Nope."

"I see. Darn." I was sorely disappointed.

It occurred to me that maybe it just had a different name—like with the tea-coffee divide—so I started to describe its characteristics, but Jude merely looked puzzled.

Before I knew it, we arrived at the workroom. We went to our separate desks, but then Jude came back over after he set down his herbs. I gave him a questioning look, and he asked me to tell him a bit more about rice. He wanted to ask his family if anyone had ever heard of it.

They were more knowledgeable about food and so forth than he was. I was quite grateful for his offer, so I told him everything I could remember.

"What are you two talking about?"

"Oh, Johan."

I had just finished describing rice in agricultural terms and was explaining to Jude that rice was a staple food in Japan when Johan walked over to us. Just like that, it wasn't only Jude and Johan listening attentively to my explanation. A whole gaggle of other researchers had gathered. Even though rice had no medicinal effects, I was talking about a plant my colleagues didn't know about—as researchers who focused on plant life, their interest was piqued.

I mean, it can't be because they're interested in learning more about a new kind of food, I thought. I was admittedly only half joking.

Jude chimed in now and again to relay the information I'd already told him.

"Rice is a grain, is it?" Johan asked.

"Yes. The food is made from the harvested seeds," I said.

"Hmm. I've never heard of it."

"Aww..." I sighed. *So even Johan hasn't heard of it—and he knows so much about plants. Now all I can do is have hope that someone in Jude's family knows something.*

At that moment, Johan had what I could only call an epiphany. "Maybe you should ask Franz about this too?"

"Why?"

"He used to travel the world a long time ago. He might've heard something."

Hm. Well, coffee came from another country. Maybe rice was grown in another country as well. It seemed entirely possible that as an experienced merchant, Franz would have researched the products of every place he visited while he traveled. Could I afford to get my hopes up for this?

As soon as work finished, I wrote a letter to Franz. To my delight, I received a reply a mere few days later. On the same day, I also received a response from Jude's family. Interestingly, both had the same answer.

"Morgenhaven?" I said aloud as I read the letter.

"It's a harbor city to the east," said Johan, who happened to be nearby.

Ah, right—I had learned about the place during one of my lectures at the palace. I had thought it sounded familiar, but I hadn't been able to place it.

"If I remember correctly, it's famous for trade, isn't it?" I asked.

"That's right. I'm surprised you know."

"I learned about it in one of my classes. I don't think about it often or anything."

Franz wrote that he had once seen a grain similar to the one I described, but it had a different name in a country to the east. Morgenhaven brought imported goods from that country to Salutania. Typically, they shipped only goods that the kingdom had requested, but there was a chance that the latest convoy had brought rice to sell as well.

Similarly, a member of Jude's family wrote that they had seen a similar kind of grain in Morgenhaven before, though they didn't remember its name.

Taking both letters into account, it seemed highly likely that both Franz and Jude's family member were talking about the same kind of plant.

Hm. I guess for now I could ask Jude's family to order the grain for me? I'd asked them to get different ingredients for me before, so we had an arrangement.

Just then, Johan piped up with his own idea. "How about you take a trip to Morgenhaven yourself?"

Huh? Wait, can I really do that?!

◆◆◆

Morgenhaven was a seaside port city in the eastern region of the Kingdom of Salutania. It was surrounded by a surplus of hills, so we didn't actually even see it until we had crested the tallest of those surrounding slopes.

I leaned out the window of the carriage to get a look at the peaceful city. The coachman stopped so I could drink in my fill.

The city was built on a bunch of smaller hills, and its roads rose up and down over them. It seemed like it might be a bit difficult to traverse.

I looked toward the harbor to find a number of moored sailing vessels. A bit out to sea, a ship unfurled its great white sails. Was it on its way in or out?

"We'll be there soon," Jude said from his seat across from mine as I took in the sights.

"Yeah..."

I ducked back in and straightened my posture with a nod. The carriage started to move again.

It had only been a week since Johan had suggested we go to Morgenhaven. We'd decided it would be a bit of an extended vacation. Johan had insisted we take our time, as I hadn't taken any days off since I started working for him.

I thought that was a bit of a misleading claim, mind you. It wasn't that I hadn't taken any days off, it was just that everyone at the institute told me that what I chose to do on those days couldn't be considered relaxation. But even if I spent those days making cosmetics for myself, cooking, and reading books in the palace library—I mean, that was all plenty relaxing, if you asked me.

However, I found it hard to resist the dream of actually finding rice, so I'd decided to take Johan up on his offer.

Thus, this time I was traveling with Jude, as he was terribly interested in other countries. Several knights from the Third Order were accompanying us as well. They weren't coming for vacation but for work—specifically, they were with us as our escorts.

Unlike in Japan, the kingdom was plagued by not only monsters but bandits. The main roads were well maintained by the lords of each domain, and they were relatively safe. However, that didn't mean they were completely free from danger. Therefore, the knights were assigned to be our escort while we traveled. For the record, the escort had been the palace's idea, but I was grateful to have them, so I had readily accepted.

Speaking of knights, Albert wasn't with us this time. I had been hoping he would come, but unfortunately, he had been compelled to stay behind at the palace. He was a knight commander, after all, and had a ton of work he needed to attend to in the capital. He had come to see us off before we left and looked incredibly disappointed that he couldn't join us.

To be honest, I had a feeling there was another reason he wasn't able to accompany us—one that was even more pressing than his other responsibilities. You see, I was going on this trip not in my capacity as the Saint but in disguise...as a regular person.

Why? Because things always had to be all ceremonious and extravagant when I conducted myself as the Saint! In order to avoid that rigmarole, we were pretending to be a group of merchants. Even the members of our knight escort were disguised as mercenaries.

If we had tried to sneak Albert into that group, the jig would have been up in no time flat. We'd just look like a bunch of nobles trying extremely hard to travel incognito. Albert just gave off this, this *sparkly* aura. There was no suppressing it, even if you dressed him up like a mercenary. That was, in my opinion, the biggest reason Albert had been forced to stay behind.

Well, if he couldn't come with us, I wanted to buy him something unusual from abroad to bring back as a souvenir, even if we couldn't find rice. Of course, I planned to buy things for Johan and the other researchers too.

"Are you sure I don't look too weird?" I asked Jude. It wouldn't be long before we reached Morgenhaven, so I checked my appearance, which I normally never did. I was in disguise, after all. Black hair and black eyes was an unusual color combination in the kingdom, so I was wearing a wig and glasses in order to hide both.

I peered into the hand mirror Jude gave me and studied the woman who stared back at me. She had brown hair and wore glasses. The glasses didn't have corrective lenses, and they felt a bit uncomfortable on my nose. It had been so long since I had last worn anything like these spectacles. All in all, it wouldn't do much to disguise me from people who already knew me, but it was fine. I was just wearing a wig of a common hair color so I wouldn't stand out as much.

It wasn't long before the coach entered Morgenhaven, and we soon arrived at the inn where we were planning to stay.

We had been sitting for a long time at that point, so I was eager to get out and stretch my stiff limbs. Jude, who had been sitting across from me, got out first. When I moved to follow, someone held their hand out to me.

Is Jude helping me out of the coach?

I took the proffered hand and looked up to say thank you, but then I froze.

"Welcome to Morgenhaven."

"Oscar?"

It was Oscar, as in the merchant guy from my company. What was he doing here?

My confusion was no doubt apparent, as he hastily explained himself while he helped me out of the carriage.

Oscar had come to Morgenhaven for business reasons, but he had heard that I was coming to search for some kind of ingredient and rushed over to catch us.

"As I knew you were here, I just had to say hello," he concluded.

"You really didn't have to go out of your way like that," I said.

"But I must. It's all because of you that we have such a successful shop."

You're exaggerating. I didn't say that out loud, but I couldn't help but make a face. I chuckled awkwardly, but Oscar showed no sign of letting that bother him. That same smile remained fixed on his face.

Jude had gone ahead and told the inn we had arrived while I was talking to Oscar, so it was time to be shown to our rooms. For some reason, Oscar accompanied us. I thought that was strange, but it turned out that Oscar was staying at the same inn.

"This is a great establishment. It's clean, and the meals they serve are delicious," Oscar said.

"Is that so?" I said.

Hooray, food! Though I'm not sure how much I can trust that statement, I thought as I recalled what Salutanian fare was generally like. I'd worry about that later, though. For now, I followed after the inn employee.

We were shown to the doors farthest down the hall on the second floor. The room on one side was for a knight and the other one was for Jude—the knight was staying next door as our full-time guard.

"And this is your room."

The employee opened the very last door, so I thanked him and followed him inside.

Uh... I froze. The room was far bigger than I had imagined. *This is considered a pretty fancy room, right? Is it okay for me to be in here? Can I touch anything?!*

I looked at the employee worriedly, and he smiled at me. From that smile, I understood that this was indeed the room that had been reserved for me. I smiled sheepishly back at him.

"I hope you have a pleasant stay." He bowed and took his leave.

For now, I'll go ahead and unpack my things. However, I had only really brought clothes that needed to be hung in the closet, so I was done pretty quickly.

Just as I finished, there was a knock at the door. Jude identified himself when I asked who it was, so I opened it for him.

"Whoa, this room is huge!"

"Did you come to check it out?"

"I confess, I was curious. My room's pretty big too, so I wanted to see what yours was like."

"Ah. So? Is mine bigger than yours?" I moved out of Jude's way so he could take in the whole room.

Jude took a single step inside to look around. Then he said with admiration, "This room is *huge*. I bet it's the biggest one in the whole inn."

"What? Really?!" I was shocked. We were disguised as regular merchants—so why was I in such a nice room?

"Yeah, yeah, it's fine." Jude casually dismissed my worry.

"But we can't just—"

"Ladies from well-to-do merchant families do stay in rooms like these on occasion."

Just how well-to-do were we talking here? Whoever stayed in a room like this had to be pretty well-off indeed. I squinted suspiciously at Jude, but he didn't say anything more.

Once he was satisfied with what he'd seen, we headed to the dining room on the first floor. We had agreed ahead of time that we would reconvene after we put our luggage away so that we could talk through our plans.

At the bottom of the stairs, I spotted the knights who

had come with us. For some reason, Oscar was with them too. We walked over to them, and Oscar waved.

"Are you taking a break?" I asked.

"No, I was waiting for you guys."

Did he have some kind of business with us? I tilted my head to the side questioningly, and Oscar told us something quite interesting: "A ship carrying imported food just arrived today."

"Really?"

"You're here in search of a type of grain from overseas, correct? It turns out that this ship was carrying grains as well."

What luck! I struck a victory pose in my mind.

Meanwhile, Jude asked just what kinds of grains the ship had brought. Unfortunately, Oscar didn't have any specific identifying information—he couldn't describe them or anything. However, he did tell us that he had heard one kind was a staple food overseas, which made me all the more hopeful.

Since the ship had only just arrived, its goods would probably be available at the morning market the following day, so we decided that we would head over to check it out at that time. The ship had reportedly brought a ton of different types of food in addition to the grains, so I was really looking forward to it.

In any case, we were planning to stay in Morgenhaven for a few days, so if we didn't see the ship's food for sale the next morning, then surely it would be on the market before long.

Oscar promised us that, in between his business obligations, he would look into things that we might not be able to find at the market. I was grateful for his help, especially as he said that if I needed anything not readily available, he could order it for me himself. I told him I'd love to take him up on that offer if the situation presented itself.

After that discussion, we all headed back to our rooms for the evening to recover from the long days of travel.

◆◆◆

The morning air was crisp and clear. However, when we reached the market, which was thronged with crowds of people, that clean, simple feeling vanished. The sun had only just risen, but the market was bustling, and the hot air was intense.

I knew that mornings started early for people in this world, but I was still amazed to see so many people gathered so soon after dawn.

"This is quite a crowd. Practically as many as I would expect to see in the capital."

"Morgenhaven is the largest trading port in the kingdom. There's probably even more people than usual since that new ship arrived yesterday. People want to see what it brought."

"Ah, yeah. That makes sense."

We had more or less the same agenda; we intended to keep coming back early in the morning until we found out what was on that ship. No matter how surprised I was by all the people, I couldn't say anything if I was doing the same thing they were.

I chatted with Jude while we walked around the market. As one would expect from a trading port, the market had tons of goods I had never seen in the capital, all of them sitting on display for sale. Every new thing caught my attention, and Jude had a hard time keeping up with me. I realized I'd been haring off in different directions without warning pretty much nonstop when Jude finally latched on to my arm.

"Hey, stop wandering all over the place."

"Sorry, sorry. There are just so many interesting things here, I keep heading toward them without thinking."

"Well, think a little more!"

I apologized to the exasperated Jude again before turning my attention back to the items on sale. I didn't want to annoy him any more than I had, so now whenever something new caught my eye, I told Jude before going over to it. We ended up trading general knowledge about our different worlds as we walked, which was surprisingly fun.

"The perishable foods here aren't all that different from what we can find in the capital. Is the only difference the cost?" I asked.

"Yeah, I think the local specialties here are cheaper."

"And the only imports I've seen thus far are things like handicrafts."

"They're interesting just to look at."

"They really are."

Specifically, we had found textiles woven with patterns I had never seen in Salutania, so they were fascinating to examine. My eyes jumped from cloth to cloth, but in the end, we were still looking for food first and foremost. Now wasn't the time to let other things distract me.

So, we returned to our food search, but we came up empty yet again. I did see some teas, though, as well as coffee and sugar. Everything was being sold for a much cheaper price than could be found in the capital, so I was tempted to make some purchases. *If we can't find what we're here for, maybe I'll just buy those instead.*

"Hmm, I don't see any rice," I said.

"You don't?" Jude asked.

"Nothing new. Speaking of, have you seen anything unloaded from that ship that just came in?"

"I don't know. I wasn't really paying attention. Should we ask one of the shopkeepers?"

"Good idea."

We had reached the end of the market, and while we had seen lots of wheat and barley, we hadn't seen anything that looked like the kind of grain that would have come from another climate. There was a possibility that we had just missed it, so asking around was definitely the way to go.

Just as we turned, I heard what sounded like people quarreling. I stopped and turned again to see a ring of men on the wharf. "I wonder what's going on there."

Jude also stopped and frowned at the ring. "Is it an argument?"

The knights who were guarding us from a short distance away had noticed the disturbance as well, and they came over to us.

I strained my eyes to see what was going on. At the center of the ring stood a tall man who was facing down the other men with a grim look on his face. He had long, black hair that was held back in a ponytail. I'd heard that black was an unusual hair color in Salutania, so he was probably a foreigner. The words "treated" and "mage" floated over to us.

"I wonder if someone's injured," I said out loud.

"What do you mean?" asked one of the knights.

"It sounds like someone needs treatment."

"I heard there was an accident on the docks yesterday."

"What kind of accident?"

"Some stacked crates fell over and someone got pinned beneath them." The knight had overheard people talking about it in the dining room at the inn this morning.

"You can understand what that guy is saying?" Jude asked.

"Yeah. Why do you ask?"

The knight frowned. "Huh. Well, you see, that tall fellow over there isn't speaking Salutanian. I suspect he's fallen back into his native language due to stress."

As a result, the people he was talking to were at a loss, as they were having trouble understanding him.

For myself, I hadn't noticed he wasn't speaking Salutanian at all. After my summoning, I had been granted the gift of being able to understand pretty much all the languages of this new world.

Well, if someone's injured... Given that man's expression, it might be a race against time. I should pitch in.

"Wait, Sei!" Jude cried out, but I ignored him and headed toward the ring of people.

The knight also tried to stop me, but I raised a hand to stop him.

Don't worry. I'm not going to do anything silly.

"Shall I interpret for you?" I asked one of the men when he noticed my approach.

He smiled with a nod, no doubt relieved that someone might be able to help.

I then looked up at the man who was having trouble communicating. His reddish-brown eyes met mine. He was a full head taller than me, and though he eyed me with due suspicion, I smiled to reassure him.

"Who are you?" he asked.

"How do you do? My name is Sei. Would you like me to interpret for you?" I asked, focusing on making myself speak the words of his language.

"You know the language of my country?! Yes, please do!"

Yes! It worked as I'd hoped it would. This translation perk sure was handy.

From that point forward, I conveyed the tall man's meaning to the people gathered around us, though I was met with concerned looks. The tall man was alarmed when they shook their heads, and he looked at me pleadingly.

I wasn't too surprised by their reaction, though. This fellow was looking for a mage, after all.

It turned out that the rumor about the accident on the docks was true. The person who had been hurt was one of this man's crew. Several people had been injured, actually, but one in particular had been gravely wounded. He had imbibed a potion, but his condition hadn't really improved. Therefore, the black-haired man, who was the ship's captain, was looking for a mage who could use Healing Magic.

However, while Morgenhaven had alchemists, no mages resided in the city. That was pretty normal, given the way mages were organized in Salutania. Every mage proficient enough in Healing Magic to be able to heal serious injuries lived and worked at the palace, and they rarely left the Assembly unless they were on a monster-slaying expedition.

I explained this to the captain, and his brow furrowed as he looked down at the ground. The locals regarded him with real pity, and the ring gradually dispersed. They knew there was nothing they could do to help.

Hmm. It's true that there are no regular mages who can use Healing Magic in Morgenhaven. However...

I glanced at Jude, who vehemently shook his head. Our knight escort wore dour looks as they slightly waved their hands to signal their own disapproval.

I'd had a feeling they'd take that stance. Chances were that I could heal this injured crewman. However, people would be bound to talk if I healed an injury that severe.

Jude and the knights were trying to stop me because they were well aware of the uproar I could inadvertently cause.

I understood this as well, of course. I only hesitated because I had already involved myself. I knew I could help, and the thought of leaving without doing so pained me greatly. I desperately wanted to do something.

After mulling it over for a moment, I sighed and raised my head. "Um, can I ask you something unrelated?" I asked the captain in his native language.

"Yes?"

"Did you use a mid-grade HP potion?"

"That's right. I asked for the most effective kind of potion they had and that was what they gave me."

"I see."

That was lucky. Lucky for me or for him, you ask? For him, of course! He must have had some good karma. You see, since he said that he had used a mid-grade HP potion, I could get away with giving him something a little special.

I fished around in the bag I had slung around my shoulder and took out a potion, which I handed to him. He looked at the vial in confusion.

"What's this?" he asked.

"Another HP potion. I carry it around with me just in case, but feel free to use it on your crew member, if you'd like. I hope it'll help him feel better."

He probably assumed I was giving it to him for my own peace of mind. He paused for a moment, and then, wearing a smile that made him look like he was on the verge of tears, he said, "Thank you."

I waved and headed back to where Jude and the others were waiting for me.

"Sei..." Jude said in a tone that made it sound like he had more to say, but I shrugged and urged him to start heading back in the direction we had come from.

I didn't say anything until we had gotten far enough away from the wharf that the black-haired captain couldn't hear me anymore. "I didn't use any magic! I just wanted to help a little... Hopefully that's enough to help the poor guy get through the worst of it."

"Let me guess, that potion was..." Jude didn't finish his sentence.

I chuckled sheepishly.

The potion I'd handed the captain was indeed a potion I kept in my bag just in case—a high-grade HP potion made by my own hand. If that wasn't enough to help the injured fellow, he really would need Healing Magic.

In my defense, I figured that even if any of these guys realized the potion I'd given them was unusually potent, I could claim that was because it was high-grade stuff. And if someone tried to say that it was stronger than a *normal* high-grade potion, I could feign ignorance and say I'd inherited it from my parents—sorry, don't know the details!

It was the least I could do, if I couldn't use magic. I hoped my escorts would overlook it.

◆ ◆ ◆

After the commotion on the wharf, we asked around with some of the shopkeepers, but the only unusual staples we heard of were wheat and beans. No rice to speak of.

However, we heard that the goods from the new ship—which turned out to be the same one that had suffered an accident—still hadn't been put on the market, so we decided to come back again the next day.

We quietly went back to the inn and stayed there until morning.

As I was eating breakfast with Jude and Oscar in the dining room, we heard a commotion coming from the entrance to the inn. We looked over and saw the black-haired captain we had met the day before walking over to us, grinning ear to ear.

I glanced around and everyone seemed to have stunned looks on their faces; no one seemed to recognize the guy. A moment later, he reached our table.

"So, this was the inn you were staying at!" the captain said in his native tongue.

"Uh," I said eloquently.

"Excuse me, but do you have some business with the lady?" Oscar stood as he spoke, sliding between the captain and me. To my surprise, he spoke the man's language as well. I was also impressed by how smoothly Oscar acted at the drop of a hat—it was like I actually was just a well-to-do lady.

He was probably being cautious because of the captain's sudden approach. Oscar was smiling, but he had a sharpish aura.

The captain was surprised by this attitude for a moment, but he immediately straightened his posture and offered his name and affiliation. His name was Ceyran, and he was the captain of the ship that had come from a country called Zaidera.

The potion I had given him yesterday had worked so well that his crew member had been able to get right back to work. The fellow's legs had been so terribly injured that they would have had to have been amputated if not for the potion. Thus, Ceyran had been searching for me ever since. The potion's power had made clear just how valuable it was, and I had given it to him for nothing.

I was relieved I'd been able to do something, especially as if I hadn't, someone might have lost their legs. If they had already performed the operation, a potion wouldn't have been enough to heal the man.

"I wanted to express my gratitude again," Ceyran said. "Thank you."

"I'm just glad I was able to help." I smiled.

I assumed that would be the end of the conversation, but there was more. Ceyran entreated us to let him pay for the cost of the potion. "It was incredible. I simply must give you something in return."

"Um..." I was at a loss. I'd figured that if anything, he would ask why it had been so effective—I hadn't imagined that he would actually want to *pay* for it.

Technically, I had kept the potion on my person just in case, but really, I had taken it because the institute had way, way too many of them, and it probably wouldn't be used if I didn't. I hated the idea of anyone giving me money for such a thing.

Furthermore, the high-grade potions I made weren't even available on the market, so they didn't technically have a price to begin with. Could I ask for compensation on the level of a regular high-grade HP potion? Oof, I had the feeling that if I did, it might cause some kind of problem later.

I had no idea what to do. Thankfully, Oscar saved the day. "As it turns out," he said, "that potion was one the master had specially prepared for my lady."

"Is that so?" Ceyran asked.

"Indeed. As for its worth, I believe we will have to ask for quite a considerable sum."

"Ah, well, if the money I have on hand is insufficient, then I will make up the difference after we have finished selling our cargo."

"That would be acceptable. However, my lady is quite generous of heart and would feel guilty for receiving any additional compensation."

I listened to the exchange nervously, but Oscar managed to arrive at a good compromise. Ceyran would let us peruse his cargo, and if there was anything we wanted, he would sell it to us at a significant discount.

Ceyran readily agreed to this, and we decided to head straight for his ship. Oscar's proposal helped us out a bunch, as we had actually been waiting for Ceyran's cargo to be put on the market.

When we got to the docks, we boarded the ship and were shown to the storeroom, which was where all of the cargo had been moved after the accident. It was dimly lit and chilly inside, as if magic had been cast there to keep it cool. I rubbed my arms against the chill as I followed the captain. The goods they had brought were things they were planning to sell in Salutania, so it was mostly wheat. Unfortunately, I had assumed this would be the case.

"Um, do you have any specialty products from your own country?" I asked.

"Specialty products? Hmm, we have a few but not that much. I'm afraid they don't sell very well here."

Ceyran led us to a corner of the storeroom where he showed us spices used in Zaidera: chili pepper, sansho pepper, and star anise. I started getting excited, seeing all these spices I recognized from Japan. These were all spices used in Chinese cuisine! If they had these, then maybe I really could hope that they had rice.

My hope bore fruit. When I asked if Ceyran had anything else from home, he brought us to another corner, where I finally laid eyes on my prize.

"Rice!" I gasped so loudly that all three men with me jumped in surprise. But in that moment, I didn't care what anyone else thought—all I cared about was the glorious fact of the rice in front of me.

"You have heard of rice, my lady?" Ceyran asked cautiously.

"Yes!"

I responded with such energy that Ceyran was a bit taken aback. However, he swiftly recovered himself and answered all my questions. As it turned out, rice was a staple food in some regions of Zaidera. Hardly anyone in the Kingdom of Salutania imported it, so Ceyran was surprised I recognized it. I surreptitiously tensed up at that observation.

"I, ah, I read about it in an encyclopedia," I said. He seemed to accept that answer for now.

Ceyran and his crew hadn't thought that they'd actually be able to sell the rice, so they hadn't brought that much of it with them, but I told him I'd like to go ahead and buy as much as he'd let me. After all, I had no idea when they would be back again.

Given my enthusiasm, Ceyran promised he would bring even more rice the next time he came to Morgenhaven, and Oscar began business negotiations without a moment's delay.

"He's amazing," I whispered to Jude.

"Yeah."

I was left thunderstruck by how quickly they came to a deal about not only the rice but the spices as well. Furthermore, Oscar leveraged my gift of the potion to haggle Ceyran down considerably. He truly was skilled at this sort of thing.

"Excuse me."

"Yes?"

We looked toward the new voice to find a boy behind us, carrying a tray. He had the same black hair as Ceyran, so he might have been from the same country. He looked to be about the same age as Liz and Aira, though my guess was that he was a member of the crew.

Several steaming mugs sat on his tray. I looked from the cups to the boy in confusion, and he shyly started handing them out. "It's so cold in here, so I thought you might like some soup to warm yourselves up."

"Thank you!" I accepted the cup and grasped it with both hands, reveling in its warmth. It brought a smile to my face.

The boy then introduced himself. He was indeed a member of Ceyran's crew—and he was actually the person who had avoided terrible misfortune thanks to my potion. A feeling of incredible relief washed over me when I realized I'd been able to help this young boy escape having both his legs amputated. He kept bowing his head while thanking me. I had a bit of a hard time getting him to finally stop.

By the time I did get him to stop, the mug had warmed my palms considerably. The hot soup was finally at a decent temperature to drink. I bent my head to take a sip but stopped when the smell of the soup hit me.

This smell...

We were in a dimly lit storehouse, so it was hard to make out what the soup actually looked like, but I *knew* this fragrance. My heart leapt with hope as I took a sip. Oh! It had been so long since I had tasted this flavor.

My nose went numb, and the corners of my lips quivered. I held back the tears threatening to overflow from my eyes and took another sip.

"This is a soup from the land of my birth. Do you like it?" the boy asked in his native Zaideran.

"Yes. It's delicious," I responded in his tongue. And then in Salutanian, I asked Jude, "What do you think, Jude? Do you like it?"

"Yeah. It's got a peculiar taste, but it's good."

"He said he likes it too," I interpreted for the boy.

The boy beamed. "Really?"

"This flavor really is unusual. What did you make it with?" Jude asked.

I conveyed Jude's question to the boy, and he answered shyly, "We use a seasoning called miso."

Miso soup. It had been so long since I had last tasted it. Although it didn't make me feel *quite* so homesick that I cried.

The boy assured us that this kind of soup tasted much better back in his hometown. He had just quickly whipped this together. Jude was nevertheless terribly impressed.

I bet the boy was right, though. Compared to the miso soup I had enjoyed back in Japan, this soup, for which he had just melted miso in hot water, did lack a bit in flavor. However, it was still delicious, especially since it had been so long since my last taste.

The Saint's Magic Power is Omnipotent

Behind the Scenes I

THERE WAS A KNOCK on the door to the king's office. The prime minister answered it, and the door opened. A young man stepped into the room.

"Special Service Agent Oscar Dunckel, reporting for duty."

"Thank you for coming. Take a seat."

This Oscar was the same young man who served as an assistant to the chairman of Sei's company. He had worn the clothes of a wealthy merchant to meet Sei at the Research Institute of Medicinal Flora, but now he was outfitted as a knight. He carried himself differently as well—he was the very image of a knight.

At the prime minister's prompting, Oscar headed to the king's desk.

"Did the meeting go well?"

"Yes. Without a hitch. The Lady Saint happily agreed to start her own company."

"Excellent." The prime minister nodded in satisfaction at Oscar's report.

At a glance, this new company looked like it would be spearheaded by Johan Valdec, the head researcher at the Research Institute of Medicinal Flora. However, the king and the prime minister were the real power behind its establishment. Everyone working at the company was affiliated with the palace, including Oscar.

"Did Franz agree to join as well?" the prime minister asked.

"He'll be the chairman," Oscar confirmed.

"We can rest easy knowing everything is in his hands."

The king sagged as if a tremendous weight had been lifted from his shoulders. Franz was profoundly loyal to the royal family, and his abilities had been proven time and again. Both the king and prime minister had utmost faith in him.

Franz had a unique history; as a younger man, he had been the king's personal spy, but his brilliance had led to his recruitment by the Special Service, i.e., the kingdom's most uniquely skilled forces. He had served as an agent, just like Oscar did now.

"Did Franz manage to recruit any of his old crew?" the king asked.

"Indeed he did. Several joined the company at Franz's invitation."

A number of people who had also once been part of the Special Service or otherwise affiliated with them were now reemployed as part of the company. Those in the Special Service had long since proved their loyalty to the royal family, and they all possessed the skills required to manage an operation like this.

The palace had gone to such lengths to establish a company full of people loyal to them, starting with Franz and Oscar, for a specific reason. In short, Johan Valdec had reported that certain people were trying to take over the company with which Sei was affiliated.

The cosmetics Sei created were incredibly popular with the noblewomen of Salutania. Even the king and his associates knew that her products flew off the shelves. They also knew that the company selling her products had a close relationship with Johan's family, House Valdec.

House Valdec had been allowed to manage this business because they were entrusted with the Saint's safety. They had no sinister designs on using the Saint for their own personal gain, and they ensured an appropriate percentage of the profits went straight back to Sei.

The noble families attempting to overtake the company in question were different. These individuals had never even tried to conceal the fact that they used and abused people for their own ends.

House Valdec had handled them thus far, but Johan suspected this would become more difficult in the near future. Agreeing with his prediction, the king and his associates had decided to take matters into their own hands.

At present, while the palace was preparing their intercession, talks between House Valdec and their rival families had already started to turn sour. One could say that their prediction had been spot on.

The king's strategy was to establish a new company that would divert attention away from the company with which House Valdec enjoyed a close relationship. Of course, Sei would be the owner of the new company, and as such, House Valdec's rivals would be left unable to complain about their unfair influence on her. It was only natural that the owner of a company should enjoy the benefits of the products she herself had devised and sold.

Also, as the Saint's social status was equal to that of the king's, the palace was ready to assume that no nobles would openly try to take her company with the same underhanded means they had been attempting to use against House Valdec.

Sei had no interest in status symbols and power; she could not be bribed with court rank or land. In any other situation, she would have firmly refused to become the owner of a company. However, the palace knew she would agree, if reluctantly, once they told her that the nobility would leave her old company alone if she were to accept ownership of the new one.

Their prediction was again correct. Sei had agreed.

Now that they had the go ahead to create the company, they had to hire employees. They rapidly came up with a plan of action. As a number of nobles had plotted to try and usurp control of the original company, they decided that all the employees of the new one would have some kind of affiliation with the palace.

In brief, Sei's knowledge was a precious commodity. Her knowledge of cosmetics alone had already made a significant impact on the kingdom's economy. If her knowledge inadvertently fell into the hands of an unscrupulous noble, there was no telling what might happen next. The palace was dearly interested in preventing this from happening and had thus devised a way to protect her by ensuring that everyone who worked at her company was one of their handpicked agents.

Among the employees, they also included personal guards for Sei. While these individuals would perform their duties in service to the company, their primary objective would be protecting the Saint.

This was already more or less the case. Wherever Sei went—to the research institute, the dining hall, and elsewhere—guards followed in her wake. Up until this point, Johan had handled all the Saint's business interactions, but from now on, Sei would be doing so on her own. Therefore, she needed guards in these situations as well.

"Excellent," said the king. "Now, I pray you will continue to watch over the Saint. Remain alert. Should anyone suspicious approach her, intervene at once."

"As you command, Your Majesty." Oscar bowed and left the office.

Once the doors closed and Oscar was out of hearing, the king let out a deep sigh.

The palace moved quickly once they received Sei's consent to establish the company. They decided where the new shop would be located, and Franz and Oscar were both busy getting it ready to open.

"Franz, here are the items you asked for."

"Thank you."

In the chairman's office on the second floor of the shop, Oscar handed over the documents he had been asked to deliver. They had come for Franz from a palace official, and they included various permits and licenses required for founding a new company.

Franz scanned the documents while Oscar sat himself down on one of the sofas.

"How have our dear 'customers' been behaving?" Oscar asked.

"It seems like they're employing a wait-and-see approach."

"Ah."

They were talking about the nobles who had meddled in the previous company's affairs. The nobles who had heard about the new company had begun investigating it. Although the company had yet to be formally founded, they had earned a fair amount of attention. It was known that they would be taking over a certain line of skincare products at the height of their popularity, and it was generally agreed that this new company was about to dominate the beauty care industry.

Franz and Oscar hadn't gone around advertising that the owner of this new company was the Saint, but it didn't take much probing to find out the truth. That was the point at which most nosy nobles dropped their investigations.

But there were exceptions—individuals who wanted to take advantage of the inevitable chaos that came with starting a business in order to steal confidential information, for one. Franz had thus far been able to thwart their plots—as well as to find out which families had sent which agents—and he had done so with aplomb.

Franz seemed to suddenly remember something, and he extracted a bundle of documents from the locked drawer of his desk. "Oh, yes. Could I ask you to deliver these for me?"

Oscar took the bundle, and as he scanned the top few documents, a surprised smile crossed his face. "Oh, Franz, quick as always," he said with no small amount of wonder.

"Why, thank you."

The documents Oscar held were itemized lists of the illegal doings of the aforementioned nobles who just couldn't let things go. He had even included, in detail, the location of a cache where proof of their illegal activities could be found. Franz might have retired, but his abilities hadn't faded in the slightest.

Thanks to this list, we should be able to take care of these nobles, Oscar thought as he rolled the documents in his hand. *But in order to do that, we need to seize the evidence.*

ACT 3
Food from Foreign Countries

THOUGH THE AVENUE by which I'd found it had been unexpected, I had finally managed to find rice. We'd only been in Morgenhaven a couple of days, so we still had a few days left before we were to return to the capital.

During that time, we were able to search the markets for any other unusual imports, but we stopped doing that soon enough. We just kept finding so many different goods in the cargo Ceyran had brought.

And here I'd assumed that it would take me forever to track down all these spices—I'd already managed to find a ton that I had half given up on ever tasting again. Ceyran had thanked me for that potion, but now I was the one who wanted to prostrate myself to him in gratitude.

How should I spend the rest of our trip? I wondered.

I wound up deciding to use my newly acquired spices to cook.

Based on the spices Ceyran and his crew had brought, the cuisine in Zaidera likely resembled Chinese food from my world. Therefore, I gathered the spices with which I would be able to whip up some fairly rudimentary Chinese cuisine. It went without saying that gathering all these ingredients had put me in the mood for it.

Okay, time to cook!

However, Jude insisted that I had to wait. Honestly, he didn't even have to try to stop me. The fact was that I simply *couldn't* cook anything. We were traveling, and I couldn't expect to borrow our inn's kitchens. Thus, I would have to wait a bit longer.

"My lady, are you interested in the cuisine of Zaidera?"

"Oh, I am!"

Two days after we first visited Ceyran's ship, he visited us at the inn and asked me this. And *of course* I was interested. How couldn't I be?

After my enthusiastic reply, Ceyran invited us to dine at the inn he and his crew were staying at. His ship's cook could treat us to a Zaideran meal at the dining room there.

I had a feeling this offer had been made as another act of gratitude for that potion. I was starting to feel like

Ceyran was going out of his way to do too much for me, but my desire to taste his country's cuisine won out.

When I glanced nervously to see what chiding expressions Jude and the knights might be wearing, they chuckled in resignation. It seemed I had been granted permission.

I beamed as I told Ceyran that we would happily visit his inn. Even he chuckled as he told us the location.

Oh boy, if he's laughing at me too, I'm getting a bit carried away, huh? Sorry! I just can't control myself. I'm so excited that I might get to eat Chinese food for the first time in literally forever...

"Huh? Has something happened, my lady?" Oscar asked as he arrived at the inn. He had bumped into Ceyran and I talking in the entrance hall.

I told him that we had been invited for dinner. Oscar seemed interested in getting to try foreign cuisine too, and he asked if he could join us. Ceyran readily agreed.

I felt a bit presumptuous—it seemed I was going to be bringing a lot of guests to dinner. *Me, Jude, Oscar, and the knights. That really is a number of folks.*

Despite their resigned laughs before, Jude and the knights also seemed intrigued by Zaideran food.

Now that the guest list was decided, we sorted out when we would be coming.

There'll be so many of us, so Ceyran probably needs to prepare some things on his end, right? Considering how long we'll all be staying here, it's probably more realistic to expect this dinner will be two or three days from now.

Or so I thought, but Ceyran assured us that he would happily host us that very night. His crew was fairly large, so they already had generous quantities of ingredients prepared.

All right, then—tonight it is!

"Welcome, my lady," said Ceyran.

"Thank you so much for the invitation."

The dinner party was at night, but the sun hadn't yet set, so it was still fairly bright out. We had arrived a bit early to the inn where Ceyran and his crew were staying.

As we talked about what kind of food would be served, Ceyran showed us to the kitchens where our meal was being made. I felt kind of guilty because I had accidentally let it slip mid-conversation that I really wanted to see what they were up to. I worried it wouldn't be okay without the cook's permission, but Ceyran insisted that it was fine.

Really? I got all anxious as we made our way to the kitchen.

"Hey, can you come here for a moment?" Ceyran called to a man in the center of the kitchen.

The fellow trotted right over to the door. "What is it, Captain?"

"Could I ask you to let her watch you while you cook?"

The cook frowned over at me with a doubtful expression. "You mean that lady over there?"

"That's the one."

I bowed, and the man turned back to Ceyran with a look that demanded an explanation. Ceyran introduced me as one of tonight's guests, and the man's expression transformed into one of amazed comprehension. Then he broke out in a broad smile.

"You're the lass who gave us the potion, aren't you?" the cook said.

"Uh, yes, I am."

"You're more than welcome in my kitchen. So, you've got an interest in cooking then, I take it?"

"I do. I wanted to see what techniques you use in Zaidera."

"I see, I see. Well, you're welcome to watch from over there."

Moments ago, the cook had been eyeing me with suspicion, but he was all smiles now. I set foot in the kitchen as instructed and settled down in a spot where I could watch what was going on without getting in anyone's way. It was precisely the spot that the cook had pointed me to.

If our whole party had hung around, we would surely have been in the way, so Jude and I were the only ones who stayed in the kitchen. It was your typical Salutanian affair. I saw the usual array of pots and knives—the same kinds I saw everywhere else. However, a couple things stood out among the cookware: a bamboo steamer and a traditional wood-burning stove. I recognized both from my old world.

Jude was as surprised as I was. To him, both of these were likely brand-new implements. He pointed at the stove and asked the cook about it. They didn't steam food in the kingdom, so it was a bit tricky to explain it to him.

As I was going over how steam cooked food in Salutanian, the cook gave a more detailed explanation. He had guessed what we were talking about from our behavior. However, he of course offered the explanation in Zaideran, so I had to interpret for Jude.

"What are you steaming today?" I asked the cook in Zaideran.

"Bao."

"Wait, did you say bao?!"

"Yes, I believe you call them dumplings over here? We make them by stuffing other ingredients into bread dough."

Of course I knew about bao—Chinese steamed buns.

In Japan, we served them with meat or red bean paste. I'd been so bowled over by the revelation that he was making bao that the cook assumed I just didn't know what he was talking about.

"The stuffing is usually ground meat, cooked vegetables, or beans that have been boiled and mashed," the cook continued.

"There sure are a lot of different varieties."

"Quite so. Depending on the filling, bao can be considered a meal or a snack. It's a versatile food."

"What kind of bao are you making for us today?"

"We've filled them with vegetables to complement the other dishes we'll be serving tonight."

Vegetable steamed buns. I had eaten them at a Chinese restaurant before, back in Japan. They had been made with vegetable oil and seasoned with sesame oil, and they had been unbelievably delicious.

Oh, by other dishes, did he mean there would be more oily foods? Vegetable steamed buns were lighter than ones filled with ground meat, so that made sense.

The cook went on to tell me about his cookware, the other dishes he was making, and the ingredients they were using, all of which I interpreted for Jude. I'd never heard of some of the vegetables the cook was using, so it was terribly interesting to hear what he had to say.

After indulging in this mini-lecture, it was time to eat, so we left the kitchen and made our way to the dining room. On our way out, we made sure to politely give our thanks to the cook and his assistants.

I still hated to intrude while they were so busy, but I'd been able to learn how to make a kind of food I had only the fuzziest memory of, so it had been an incredibly valuable use of my time.

◆ ◆ ◆

Several round tables were set up in the dining room, and we were split up between them. I was encouraged to sit at the table farthest into the room, so Jude, Oscar, and I took our seats there. Our knight escorts were seated at another table.

I saw a number of unfamiliar faces all around. When I asked who they were, I was informed that they were the higher-ranking members of Ceyran's crew. All in all, there were a lot more people than I'd thought there would be.

A few moments later, wine was brought out to each table, though I had heard that they hadn't brought any Zaideran alcohol with them. I was curious, so I craned my neck to see what the other tables were having and found that the knights were being served ale.

As drinks were being poured, Ceyran briefly introduced me to everyone. All of his crew members beamed at me, which made me feel somewhat self-conscious.

Uh, can we—can we just move on, please?

I encouraged Ceyran to skip ahead in his speech out of sheer embarrassment. Thankfully, he soon led us in a toast, and everyone drank.

After the toast, we were brought all kinds of food—some I recognized, some I didn't. Jude and the knights were thoroughly delighted by every unfamiliar dish. The cooks had used a plentiful variety of seasonings, spices, and cooking methods. The cuisine in Zaidera was quite sophisticated.

Since we had been invited to dine, I understood that the cooks had gone all out and made much fancier fare than usual. Even the crew members were impressed with what they were being served.

The food was carried out on large platters and the people waiting on the tables served out our portions. I eagerly took my first bite, and my mouth was filled with the unique taste of a particular spice.

This must be star anise. I bet it's going to be a divisive one, I thought.

I was right. The knights had a whole bunch of different opinions.

"How do you like it?" Ceyran asked as I chewed my way through the first dish. He was sitting at my table.

"It's delicious." It was true—I'd always liked the flavor of star anise.

He smiled with relief. It seemed that he could tell that not everyone was as into it as I was. "We're quite used to the flavor, but I know a number of people from Salutania don't care for it as much. I was a bit worried you wouldn't."

"Yeah, you can really tell." I glanced toward the knights, so animated as they debated the flavor with each other, and then met Ceyran's gaze again. We exchanged a wry chuckle.

Oscar's expression had changed only very subtly at the unique taste. Jude seemed fine with it. I'd figured he would be, since he worked at the institute. Our institute was full of people who were fine with eating herbs raw, after all, so it stood to reason that he'd be unfazed by the flavor.

"Do the people of Salutania prefer food that honors the flavor of the main ingredients?" Ceyran asked.

"I think so."

"As it turns out, we've recently begun using herbs as seasoning," Oscar cut in, also speaking Zaideran.

He was definitely referring to the kind of food we made at the institute. Oscar had started making frequent visits to the institute for meetings with me about the company. He'd tried the food at our dining hall, and I suspected he had fallen in love with it. We always seemed to have our meetings around lunchtime.

"Herbs, you say?" Ceyran asked.

"Yes. They lend a most refreshing flavor."

"I see. I assume they're good for the body as well?"

"I'm afraid I haven't heard such a thing."

The fact was that all food benefited the body in some way. However, people were usually more focused on flavor than health benefits, so Oscar probably didn't know a huge amount about it.

Balanced diets... Healthy bodies... That actually reminded me of something. "Hey, Ceyran, in your country, do you have a kind of cuisine that's supposed to be especially healthy?"

He gave me just the answer I was hoping for. "We do indeed believe that there is a link between food and health, and that some foods are better for the body than others."

I reflexively leaned in and peppered him with more questions. He admitted that he didn't know all that much about it—this theory was more popular among those in higher social positions. I did remember hearing something like that before.

The subject soon went off on a tangent about herbs. Through me, Jude played an active part in this discussion. Ceyran didn't know much about the topic, but he did his best to tell us what he knew about the herbs in Zaidera. The conversation got rather technical, so Ceyran called over one of the crew members sitting at another table. This man was the ship's doctor and was therefore much more knowledgeable on the subject. He confirmed that in Zaidera, they didn't just use herbs to make medicine. They also did things like boil tree bark and drink the water.

Wait, was this like traditional Chinese medicine?

I listened to him with vested interest. The doctor asked us about Salutanian herbs as well, and we told him what we could. Between my knowledge and Jude's, we were able to give him quite an informed set of answers. When we revealed that Jude made potions for a living, he nodded in understanding.

"Is this the fellow who made the potion you gave us, then?" Ceyran asked.

Uh-oh.

"Oh, n-no, that was commissioned for me by my father. I don't know who made it," I answered, feeling a sudden chill.

Jude's smile was strangely frozen on his face. He realized we were in danger as well.

Thankfully, Ceyran didn't press for more details.

"Are you interested in learning more about that potion?" Oscar asked just as I was beginning to think we'd escaped the jaws of doom—come on, Oscar!

"Of course I am."

"Well, I did hear that Zaidera is quite advanced in the study of herbology. Do you have a similar kind of potion there?"

"Hmm, I'm not sure. Considering how powerful that potion was, I have a feeling that only people of high social status would even know if such a potion existed."

I was at my wits' end by the time that conversation ended. I was incredibly relieved that Oscar had taken over. I was sure I'd been on the verge of making a huge mess of things.

Actually, the truth was probably that I'd already made a bit of a mess. I really needed to stop talking about potions already or I'd reveal more than I already had.

Thankfully, my prayer was answered, and they started talking about life on board a ship instead. From what they said, it sounded like ship life was as hard as I'd thought it might be.

"All in all, it means daily rations on a ship are rather tragic."

"Oh, it really sounds like it." I couldn't hold back my tears. It all sounded so horrible! My sadness wasn't an act at all.

While Zaideran cuisine was wonderfully sophisticated, on a voyage, they could only eat preserved foods that lasted a long time. This meant food that had been dried or pickled in salt. Fresh vegetables and fruit rotted quickly, so even if they did bring produce aboard, they had to eat it fast.

Ceyran asked if we knew of any food in Salutania that would keep, but Jude and Oscar didn't have an answer for him. If Oscar didn't know—and he seemed like he would've—there probably weren't any known nonperishable foods other than what Ceyran was already carrying.

Preserved foods... I racked my brain, trying to remember the types of food they'd brought on long ship voyages back in my old world. *Maybe* that *kind would taste better than what Ceyran already mentioned? There are a lot of opinions on its flavor, though.*

Ceyran noticed me lost in thought. "Might you have some kind of idea, my lady?"

"Maybe, but I'm not so sure about the taste." Also, I had never made it before, so I didn't know for sure how it'd end up.

Ceyran sounded intrigued anyway and asked me if I would mind trying to make it.

It was simple enough to do so, and I had an idea of how it was done. The question was whether I could acquire the key ingredient. I decided that if I could find the ingredients at the market tomorrow, then I would make a go of it. Thus, I accepted Ceyran's request on that condition.

◆◆◆

The day after the dinner party, Jude and I headed to the market first thing in the morning. The morning market sold vegetables that had been grown locally. The freshly harvested vegetables were vibrant in the morning sun.

I agreed to Ceyran's request on the condition that I could find the ingredients, but are they actually going to have them here? Not to mention, they're only selling what they actually harvested today, so there's a chance they won't have it even if they do grow it nearby, I thought a bit uneasily as I looked around the shops. Then I spotted what I was after: cabbage. *Oh, good, they're selling it today.*

Seeing me pick up a vegetable that even commoners regularly ate, Jude tilted his head curiously. "You're going to preserve cabbage?"

"That's right."

I was going to make sauerkraut.

Cabbage was usually used in soups in the Kingdom of Salutania, so Jude had probably never imagined it could be turned into preserves. I brushed off his puzzled look and got the attention of the shopkeeper. I bought a whole ton of cabbages, since their volume would decrease when I cooked them down. I also bought salt, bay leaves, and a small cask. I asked each shop to deliver my purchases to the inn Ceyran was staying at. I would be making the sauerkraut there.

Once we were done shopping, we made our way straight to Ceyran's inn. He and his crew were just finishing breakfast, so we arrived at just the right time. Ceyran came to meet us at the entrance.

"Good morning," I sang.

"Good morning. Did you manage to find the ingredients?"

"That I did."

"Excellent. Let's make our way to the kitchen, then."

After that brief exchange, we headed into the kitchen, where I found everything I had purchased at the market along with some spices. These spices were from Ceyran's cargo, and I had told him the night before that I would need them to make this dish.

All right. He got everything I asked for. After checking the ingredients, I turned to the cooks and gave them the instructions. All I did was teach them; I didn't have a hand in the cooking this time.

"So we should finely chop all of these cabbages?"

"Yes, please do."

There were quite a few, but the chopping was done before I knew it. That's what happens when you share the work. *Just as you'd expect from people who cook for a living. Their knife work sure is speedy.*

While some cooks were chopping, others got the cask ready for the preserves. We placed the cask in the sink and poured boiling water into it. Then we left it for a bit. If we were using a glass bottle, we could've sterilized it more quickly by boiling it in a pot, but the cask was simply too big and wouldn't have fit in any available vessel. Thus we had to sterilize it this way.

"Oh, are you going to sterilize that too?" asked Jude.

"Yup. It will make the food kept inside the cask last longer."

"I see."

Everyone at the institute already understood the concept of sterilization. As in, I'd taught it to them. The world I'd come from was generally far more advanced when it came to the study of the natural sciences. Whenever I mentioned something my colleagues didn't recognize, they grilled me relentlessly, and I frequently wound up holding entire lectures about whatever topic had caught their interest.

Anyway, thanks to that, Jude already knew what I was up to with this boiling business.

A little while later, as we were pouring out the hot water, the cooks interrogated me about the reason for doing so, just like my colleagues had. I didn't actually name the concept of sterilization, but I did tell them that it would stop the food from spoiling, which they were plenty impressed with all on its own. They didn't have preserved cabbage in Zaidera, but they did preserve similar foods, and they wanted to give this technique a try with those later.

Please go ahead and make good use of this knowledge!

While we were doing this, the other cooks finished chopping up the cabbages. Now we moved on to the next steps. I directed them to dredge the finely cut cabbage slices in salt and knead them until they had pressed out all the liquid. Then I had them mix the cabbage with the prepared spices. After that, they packed the cabbage into the cask and poured the liquid that had been pressed out of the leaves on top. With that, we were done.

"Stuff it in so there aren't any gaps."

"Like this?"

"Exactly."

They did as I said. I'd read a recipe once long ago that said this would prevent the propagation of any unnecessary bacteria during fermentation.

"It's finished now?" Ceyran asked just as they were layering the outermost leaves of the cabbages on top of the mixture, followed by a stone cover for pickling.

"Yes. Now you just need to store it in a cool, dark place."

My understanding was that you were supposed to let a mixture ferment for four to six weeks, but I wasn't sure if that was accurate, as this was my first time making anything like it. I also didn't know how long the sauerkraut would be safe to eat, so I told Ceyran to make sure to keep an eye on its relative freshness.

I also, er, couldn't guarantee that it would taste good. This was my first time making sauerkraut, after all, and even back in the world I'd come from, people had been pretty divided on the taste.

When I warned Ceyran in vague terms, he chuckled dryly and said he understood.

"That was a good deal easier to make than I thought it would be," Ceyran said.

"Mm-hmm. Sorry it was the only thing I could think of, though."

"Not at all. With this, we'll have one more thing to eat on board. I'm quite grateful to you."

Sauerkraut really was the only thing I could come up with, given the types of food Ceyran's country already had. It wasn't like I could suggest pickled vegetables or food preserved in miso—they definitely already had those. There was no way they wouldn't have figured those out, considering the sophistication of the cooking I'd seen them do thus far.

"Vegetables, though... That was a blind spot," Ceyran murmured to himself.

"What do you mean?"

We had reached a good break point, and Ceyran had suggested we take our leave for a bit. I'd taken him up on that, and we were having tea in the dining room.

"When you mentioned vegetables on the ship, I imagined fresh vegetables," he explained. "I hadn't thought of bringing the kind that had already been pickled."

"Your cook did mention that you had other types of pickled vegetables."

"Indeed. Your cooking endeavors today made me wish we had brought those too."

I smiled at his words. I hadn't done all that much, but I was glad to have been of some further help to him.

"Is that pickled cabbage you made something you eat here in the Kingdom of Salutania?"

"No, it's from a foreign country I read about in a book once."

"Ah, so that's why you'd never made it before."

"Yup."

To be fair, that foreign country happened to be in a completely different world, I thought. But I could usually get away with claiming my unusual knowledge came from books.

"You must be an avid reader then," Ceyran went on, which made a cold sweat prickle down my back.

Thankfully, our conversation reached an end, so we brought our impromptu tea party to a close. I thanked Ceyran again for the dinner he had hosted the night before and then returned to the inn I was staying at.

Before I did, he told me that the next time we met, he would be sure to tell me how the sauerkraut turned out. I had to wonder if we really would ever meet again. Oscar had arranged for my company to make regular purchases of rice, miso, and the like, so I supposed there might be a chance.

Hmm, I guess I could try making sauerkraut again back at the capital? If it tastes good, then maybe we could bring it along on the next expedition.

The Saint's
Magic Power is
Omnipotent

Japanese Food

IT HAD BEEN A WEEK since we returned from Morgenhaven. I resumed my work at the institute the minute we got back. I made sure to ask a palace official if there was word of any new black swamps, but he'd heard nothing. In short, the Saint was on call but unneeded, and I was able to spend the days following our return in relative peace.

I'd already decided what I'd do the next time I had a free day: make Japanese food.

With that in mind, I dedicated myself to completing all the work that had piled up while I was away. I finally got through it all one afternoon when I had reached a good stopping point in my work.

"Today's the day, huh?" Johan asked as he came into the kitchen at the institute. I was making my preparations, and as usual, he was immediately drawn in by the prospect of a new dish.

"That's right!" I replied with a grin.

He peered curiously at my hands. "Is this the so-called rice you were looking for?"

"It is. Rice was a staple food back in Japan." My precious white rice was enshrined in a basket. I had just finished measuring it out and was going to wash the grains. "It'll be a little while before it's ready," I told him.

"Really?"

"Yeah, after I finish washing it, it needs to soak." I explained the next steps I needed to take as I washed the rice. Once I made clear just how much time it would be before I actually started cooking in earnest, Johan sighed and said he'd come back later, then went back to work.

I felt a bit unsure as I watched him walk away. I didn't know if I could actually promise a good rice dish. In Morgenhaven, I'd learned how to make it in the Zaideran style from Ceyran's cook, but I wasn't especially confident. It was just so different from how I had cooked rice back in Japan. I mean, I had always used a rice cooker; I had only made it in a pot once or twice in my life.

I'd hoped to only share my rice once I was sure I'd managed to cook it properly, but now Johan had caught me red-handed. I had no choice but to let him try whatever I made this time the moment it was ready.

I guess I'll just have to try my hardest and pray for the best.

After the rice was done soaking, I poured it and the appropriate amount of water into a pot and placed that over a flame. While I had gotten better at controlling the level of flame in the oven over the past year, I still had a ways to go. With the help of the chefs, I somehow managed to keep it going at the right intensity.

"I can smell it now," Johan said when he came back to the kitchen later.

"Yup. I think it should be done soon." I didn't have a clock, so I had to rely on sound and smell to know whether it was finished.

When I looked over my shoulder, I realized Johan wasn't my only audience member. The chefs were watching me as well—as was Jude. It was kind of a weird tableau, all of them staring so intently at the pot like that. I held back laughter as I joined in.

I think it's about time now. I increased the strength of the flame just a touch and heard a popping sound from the pot. That told me it was time to remove the pot from the flame. Now it just needed to steam.

"Is it done?" Johan asked.

"Not yet. It has to sit and cook in the steam first."

"Oh..."

"Don't look so disappointed. I'm going to start cooking another dish now."

Johan's face lit up at this. I chuckled at the sight of his shining eyes and started working. I was going to make miso soup.

I started by chopping up the same kinds of vegetables that I would when making other soups. The good thing about miso soup was that you didn't need too many ingredients. I was grateful for that, seeing as my access to ingredients was limited. I did have the ingredients to make a variety of Western-style soups if I wanted.

"You're going to make soup?" Jude asked.

"Yeah, using miso."

"You mean that stuff we drank in the storeroom?"

"Exactly. But the one we tried then was pretty rudimentary compared to what I'm going to make."

"Oh, yeah?"

"Where I come from, we dissolve the miso in soup stock made from fish, and we add other ingredients too."

"Huh." Jude sounded impressed.

The miso soup we'd had on the ship had basically been miso paste dissolved in hot water, so it had tasted a bit thin. I was making it myself now, so I wanted to try to get as close as possible to the miso I dreamed of. Thus, I had made soup stock using some small dried fish I had bought in Morgenhaven.

I'd asked one of the chefs to start the soup stock while I was working on the rice. I was unfamiliar with this kind of fish, but they managed to make a pretty good stock.

Before long, the miso soup was done, and it was finally time to check the rice. My heart raced as I lifted the lid. As I did, an inviting fragrance washed over me.

I used a rice paddle, which I had commissioned from an artisan with extra pay for a rush job, to fold the rice. The bottom was slightly crispy. I tasted it and found the grains a little soft, but this surely qualified as a success. This sweetness that I hadn't tasted in so long...it filled me with emotions that I tried to keep down deep inside.

Outwardly, I grinned, which elicited a round of cheers from the chefs.

"Did it come out all right?" Johan asked.

"I feel like it's a touch too soft."

"From the look on your face, that doesn't seem to be much of a problem."

Johan's smile was full of hope as I urged him and Jude to head out to the dining hall. The chefs and I quickly finished prepping the dishes, and then I joined them in the dining hall too. People were already murmuring as they tried the two new dishes.

I took my seat and admired the rice and miso soup all over again. We didn't have any rice bowls, so we'd just used flat dishes for the rice, and the miso soup was poured into soup bowls. However, I felt incredibly emotional. Finally, I could eat Japanese cuisine again.

My heart had fluttered when I tested the food, but now that I was really sitting down to eat my fill, that feeling grew even stronger.

"It's so good," I couldn't help but say that as I chewed the rice, its natural sweetness overtaking my taste buds.

Johan, sitting across from me, laughed genially. "I'm glad it came out so well."

"Yeah..."

Still churning with deep feeling, I reached for the miso soup. I took a sip, and the flavor of the fish stock filled my nose and mouth. The savory miso followed it up, and I let out a satisfied sigh. *Ahhh, miso soup for the soul.*

As I basked in the warmth of the soup, Jude seemed surprised. "Wait, *this* is miso soup?"

"Yup."

"This is completely different from what we had in Morgenhaven!"

The soup stock really did make a difference, just like I'd thought it would. "You think so?"

"Yeah. The kind we tried there was more, hm, sour?"

"Well, that was just miso diluted with water, so it was more the taste of pure miso."

"But you had a more complicated recipe."

"Yeah, starting with a soup stock as a base. Plus, there are vegetables to complement the flavor."

"That's why the taste isn't so strong?"

"More or less."

"I'd like to see what the miso tastes like when it's a more central flavor."

"Should I try experimenting later?"

It was unusual for Jude to be so into talking about these subtle differences; he agreed with a smile. Of course, Johan wanted to participate in this taste testing too.

After chatting for a bit, a thought suddenly occurred to Johan. "Do rice and miso have some kind of effect too?"

"What do you mean?"

"Like, do they increase our maximum HP or something?"

"Oh, you mean with my Cooking skill. I have no idea."

At times, when someone who had the Cooking skill made food, the dishes they cooked could essentially buff those who ate the dishes. I had made the food today, so if there was an effect, it would probably be obvious in short order.

At Johan's prompting, everyone at the table checked their stats simultaneously.

"At a glance, doesn't seem like anything's changed," I said.

"Yeah," Jude agreed.

"Too bad. I thought there might be one, after hearing you speak about that medicinal cooking," Johan said with some disappointment.

Honestly, I empathized with him. Miso was said to be good for your health. It seemed nearly unbelievable that it didn't have any effect. Maybe it did something that wasn't immediately obvious? Something like increasing physical attack power or natural HP recovery.

I brought that up and Johan agreed. We would have to keep checking.

I had bought as much rice and miso as I could from Ceyran, but I wasn't sure it was enough to really experiment with. How were we supposed to conduct tests when we had so few ingredients to work with?

I ate the rest of my rice while trying to come up with an effective way to go about these new experiments.

◆ ◆ ◆

"Hello!"

"Thanks for coming, Aira."

A few days after I figured out how to cook rice, Aira arrived at the institute around noon. I was planning to make another meal featuring rice that day, so I had invited her over for lunch. She had immediately agreed when she heard about the star ingredient.

The first time I'd made rice, Aira had been able to eat it that same night. I had gone to the barracks of the Royal Magi Assembly to bring her onigiri rice balls and miso soup. At first, Aira had peered curiously at the basket I handed her, but once she removed the cloth covering, her eyes opened wide. She stared up at me with surprise, and I invited her to eat them with me. The two of us enjoyed the taste of rice and miso together in her room, where we talked about our faraway homeland as we ate. As we did, the food tasted saltier than it had earlier.

"What's on the menu today?" Aira asked.

"I'm making sushi bowls."

"Like chirashizushi?! You can make that here?"

"Well, it'll taste a bit different, since the vinegar I'm using isn't rice vinegar."

"I don't care. I can't wait!" Aira smiled happily as we headed into the dining hall.

Just as I had told her, we were having sushi rice bowls with a variety of ingredients sprinkled on top. Since I had used wine vinegar instead of rice vinegar, it didn't have the precise flavor I had been expecting. Not that it tasted bad or anything—quite the contrary.

For the ingredients sprinkled on top, I used burdock root and some dried whitefish I had bought in Morgenhaven. I didn't forget to add thin strips of omelet too.

I had actually harvested the burdock from Johan's herb garden. As far as he was concerned, it was a type of medicinal herb from abroad that he was cultivating for his own research. I'd realized he was growing it about a year ago. I had been so surprised when I saw it in his harvest. However, he was even more surprised when I told him that we'd eaten the roots as a vegetable in Japan.

Now that I've found rice and miso, maybe I can ask him to grow more burdock so we can use it in cooking?

Aira and I sat down at one of the tables in the dining hall, and one of the chefs brought out the chirashizushi with a smile on her face. The chefs, with their overwhelming curiosity about food, were in a great mood today. After all, they had just had a chance to learn about a new meal that used rice.

Aira's eyes sparkled as they placed the chirashizushi and miso soup before her. She gave a hurried thanks and dug in. "I haven't eaten this since I was little..."

"Really?"

"Yeah, my mom bought it for me for Girls' Day when I was young, but I think she stopped around the time I was in first or second grade."

"Oh, yeah. My grandma made it for us for Girls' Day. She rarely made it otherwise." Tears began to well in my eyes as I thought about my grandma.

No, no. Stop. Calm down. I quietly took a deep breath to soothe myself. I didn't want anyone to notice I'd grown verklempt. To better hide my feelings, I picked up my soup bowl.

Whenever my grandma made chirashizushi, she had served it with a clear soup with other ingredients, but today we were having it with miso soup. I could probably make a clear soup using just salt and broth, but it would feel lacking without any soy sauce to add to it. *If only I had that, I could really recreate her recipe...*

Well, if miso existed in this world, there was a good chance that soy sauce did too. I would have to ask Oscar to find out whether they had any in Zaidera.

"That was delicious," Aira said with an enormous grin after she cleaned her plate.

"I'm glad."

I had been a bit worried about the flavor, given the wine vinegar, but she seemed to like it just fine.

Aira had to get back to work, so I gave her some pound cake to enjoy later before she left. Apparently, pound cake was very popular in the Royal Magi Assembly. Aira thought people might fight over it, so I handed her several loaves. She felt guilty, but it was fine—we always made a big batch.

The next day, we had an unexpected visitor at the institute.

"What in the world are *you* doing here?" I demanded.

"Why, I'd simply like to ask you something."

Grand Magus Yuri Drewes had turned up right at the beginning of the workday. Behind him stood a disconcerted-looking Aira.

I'll be honest—I recoiled at the sudden appearance of Yuri's lovely smile at that early hour. *What the heck could he want from me?!*

It would have been weird to stand around talking in the foyer, so I led them both to the parlor.

"I've come to learn more about the food Aira ate yesterday," Yuri told me as soon as he sat down on the sofa.

"You mean the chirashizushi and miso soup?"

"That's right! I would like to try that rice dish as well. Can you make it again?"

The force of that smile of his was overwhelming. I looked to Aira for an explanation, but she just shook her head as if to say she had no idea what was going on either. But she did clue me in as to what had happened.

The day before, after she returned to the barracks, she

had gone to train in the yard. Yuri had happened to pass by and spotted her practicing. He had watched her for a bit before descending to interrogate her about what she had or hadn't altered in her routine that day. In the end, Aira had told him about having lunch at the institute's dining hall.

Well, now it all made sense. If Yuri was asking to try what Aira had eaten, then he had noticed some new effect that had caught his interest. Judging from his present behavior, in all likelihood, the effect had something to do with magic. I had been planning to conduct experiments to figure out the effects of meals made with rice and miso anyway, so perhaps he could help me out a bit.

"I don't mind making it at all," I said. "But I do have a request."

"What would that be?"

"I hate to ask, but would you please let me get Johan's permission first?"

"Very well, I shall accompany you." Yuri stood up immediately. Goodness, he *really* wanted to eat that chirashizushi, huh?

I assumed we would get permission pretty much right away, so I forced Yuri to stay behind in the parlor. He didn't argue, and he seemed to be trying his best, so I was fairly sure he'd actually wait there until I got back.

I nevertheless made my way to Johan's office as quickly as I could and knocked on the door. He invited me in as he usually did, none the wiser to the situation, so I lunged through.

Johan stared in open surprise. "What's all the rush?"

Okay, I was in a tizzy—I had a good reason! "Sorry for the interruption, but I need your permission for something."

He looked concerned as I explained that Yuri wanted to eat a dish I had made the day before and that I was thinking about asking him to participate in our new food-based studies.

"Lord Drewes wants in?"

"That's right. I'm guessing this means the effect has something to do with magic...so I think it would be best if, this time, we asked for his cooperation."

"You have a point."

"Besides, we don't have much rice or miso left, so, you know, it might save us a lot of time if he helps."

"You're right that he has an exceptionally discerning eye for anything that has to do with magic... Very well, let him in on it."

You might have guessed, but I had my own reasons for asking Yuri to participate. We had a limited supply of the key ingredients, and those were hard to acquire. Selfishly,

I wanted to maximize our experimental capability in order to preserve as many leftovers as possible to treat Aira and myself to more Japanese cooking.

However, the researcher in me also thought it was important to find out the effects of these two ingredients. Therefore, I wanted to be highly strategic with our studies, and thus, it made perfect sense to fold an arcane expert like Yuri into our work. Now all I needed to do was ask Yuri to pick some qualified mages for the experiments themselves.

Armed with Johan's permission, I headed back to the parlor.

The moment I stepped back into the room, Yuri beamed like the morning sun. "Well? What did he say?"

Just how badly does he want to do this? I tensed up a touch under that brilliant grin, and it widened all the more when I revealed that we had permission to go forward.

I glanced next to Yuri to find Aira looking utterly relieved. Our eyes met, and we shared a smile of exhausted amusement.

After that, I formally asked Yuri for his help in investigating the effects of rice and miso, which he readily agreed to.

A thought suddenly occurred to me at that moment, and I suggested that maybe we should tell Lord

Smarty-Glasses about this. Aira said she would do so for me. *Thanks, Aira!*

Hopefully, as we'd done the legwork to get approval and were doing this all aboveboard, Lord Smarty-Glasses wouldn't try to stop us. Or, he probably wouldn't... Probably.

◆◆◆

Three days after Yuri's visit to the institute, we began our study on chirashizushi and miso soup.

I was surprised to hear back from him so quickly—he got back to me the same day we got permission, actually. When he said that we would conduct our survey three days later, well, the speed at which he got everything ready made me realize just how greatly he was looking forward to this.

I wonder how much trouble this caused for Lord Smarty-Glasses...

All it took was one look at his deeply furrowed brow to know the answer.

"Thanks for coming today," I said tentatively, trying to take Lord Smarty-Glasses's mood into consideration.

"And thank you for having us! I simply can't wait," Yuri replied quite cheerfully, a dazzling smile on his face.

In addition to those two, three other mages had joined us. Yuri was their leader, after all. Although usually in name only...

Lord Smarty-Glasses sighed deeply before mumbling his own, "Thank you for having us."

As I led the mages to the dining hall, I learned that they were the top five mages in the Assembly.

The top five? Doesn't that mean these are all extremely busy people?

"Um, what about your schedules? Surely you have other obligations?" I asked in surprise.

"Oh, no need to worry about that," Yuri answered casually.

Lord Smarty-Glasses sighed, and the other three mages chuckled awkwardly. Yeah, my guess was that they had all taken great pains to reorganize their schedules.

Given how dear our ingredients were, I had asked Yuri to find people skilled enough to be able to detect the effects of the food. He had indeed gone and done just that. But I was starting to feel pretty guilty for all of the trouble I had caused.

"The food is a bit sweet, a bit sour. Once you're done eating, please check for any changes in your stats."

"Understood."

"Got it."

I guided everyone into the dining hall, and just as we were getting seated, the servants brought out the food.

I was only serving them chirashizushi to start. If they had both rice and miso soup at the same time, we wouldn't be able to tell which food caused which effect, if we discovered there was one at all.

The mages looked curiously at their dishes, so I gave them a simple explanation of the contents. I warned them that the sour notes came from the vinegar. I didn't want them to innocently take a bite and assume it had spoiled. This seemed to help. They all commented on what an unusual flavor the rice had, but none of them shrank away.

"This tastes so different from anything I've had before. But I don't dislike it."

"Yeah, and I've never even seen these white grains. What do you call this food again?"

"The white grains are rice. They're from another country."

"Are they now?"

The three mages seemed to like the food well enough. I couldn't tell what Lord Smarty-Glasses thought, due to his usual total deadpan. He ate in silence, but I assumed he didn't dislike it, as his brow remained unfurrowed.

Yuri, on the other hand...

"All the food you prepare is so consistently delicious, and this dish is no exception. I bet I could eat this every day," he said, smiling radiantly.

"R-really? Thank you."

Unfortunately, we didn't have the stores to meet his request. But there was no point in mentioning that now. I kept quiet about my ingredient woes and instead asked what I wanted to know: "So, is there any change in your stats?"

"Good question. *Stats*... Nothing as far as I can tell."

Yuri was the first to check, but none of the other mages saw any changes in their stats either.

Hmm, in this case, maybe it was the miso soup that had the effect that caught Yuri's attention?

Just as I was thinking that, Yuri abruptly stood from his chair and headed outside.

"Huh? Where are you going?"

"I'd like to try something."

"Why outside?"

"Oh, it would be difficult to clean up if I did it in here." With that, he promptly left.

Everyone was dumbfounded, but we rapidly recovered ourselves and hurried after him. We found Yuri just outside in the institute gardens, already starting to cast some sort of spell. It went off before Lord Smarty-Glasses had a chance to stop him.

A sphere of water launched into the sky and burst in midair, raining droplets of water down everywhere. It was the same Water Magic spell Jude used when watering the herb garden.

"Uh..."

"It's just as I suspected." Yuri turned to us with a gleeful expression. "My magical attack power has increased."

"Huh?"

He needed to conduct further tests to verify the change, and he announced that he was heading back to the Royal Magi Assembly's practice grounds.

To be more precise, Yuri started trying to verify it right there in front of the institute, but Lord Smarty-Glasses dragged him away.

Thank you for stopping him. I'm glad no harm came to our gardens.

I asked the servants to clean up the dining hall, and then we all headed over to the Royal Magi Assembly. When we arrived at the practice grounds, Yuri was already in full spectacle mode. As he cast spell after spell, I realized that he had been holding himself back at the institute.

In order to test the effects of the food, the other mages started casting spells as well.

"*Ice Arrow.*" This was my first time seeing Lord Smarty-Glasses use magic. He shot arrows of ice that flawlessly hit the center of a target that was placed quite far away—and he did so over and over.

I wasn't the only one impressed. Others gave shouts of admiration as well.

I looked around and found that a ton of mages had gathered. I asked a nearby mage what they were all doing here, and he said that they hardly ever saw all five of the Assembly's top mages at the practice grounds at the same time, let alone all casting magic. Everyone in the barracks had come to watch.

After a while, Lord Smarty-Glasses stopped casting his ice arrows and came over to me. Out of nowhere, he said, "My accuracy seems to have increased as well."

"Really?"

"Normally, I hit a bit off the mark."

I looked back at the target. Every last one of his arrows had hit dead center. The impact marks weren't that big either, so it was plainly obvious that they had all done so.

Lord Smarty-Glasses went on to say that although he had confidence in his control over the arrows, they didn't normally converge so perfectly.

"What about your magical attack power? Grand Magus Yuri said his went up."

"That has also undoubtedly increased."

Magical attack power influenced the intensity of your magic and size of your spells. This was why Yuri's sphere of water outside the institute had covered such a wide area. Normally, the area of effect would've been a touch smaller.

Lord Smarty-Glasses also explained that he had been able to use less magic power to achieve the standard effect, which was how he had confirmed that his attack power had increased.

Based on the analysis Yuri and Lord Smarty-Glasses performed, it was pretty much settled that chirashizushi increased both magical attack power and accuracy.

The other three mages followed up with similar conclusions. I asked them to check if there were any other effects, just in case, but it seemed to be just those two.

Within a few hours, the effects of the food had worn off, so we decided to call it a day.

"Thank you for helping me today," I said.

"Don't mention it. It is I who ought to thank you for introducing me to such a wonderful new kind of food," Yuri responded cheerfully.

Most food affected physical attacks and HP. The only magic-related effect we had found thus far had impacted MP. However, in this study, we had confirmed that other magic-related effects did in fact exist. I could tell that Yuri, notorious for his magic obsession, was very much intrigued by this finding.

"It's difficult to acquire the ingredients you used in the dish you made today, yes?" Yuri asked.

"That's right."

"And here I would eat it every day if I could..."

"That would be a challenge right now. I was thinking of having the ingredients regularly imported, though."

"What do you mean?"

"You see, rice is a staple food in the country I come from, so I'd also like to be able to eat it at least once a day myself."

"In other words, once you start importing it, you *will* be able to eat it every day at the institute's dining hall?"

"Probably?"

"Is that so? Then please let me know the moment that happens. And allow me to join you!"

I didn't think he'd actually go that far! I wouldn't be surprised if he really did start coming every day. But whatever. I'll make sure the Royal Magi Assembly gets charged for his meals. Either way, I told Yuri that I would, and as I did so, he smiled even more brilliantly than before.

Behind the Scenes II

IN A ROOM at an inn in Morgenhaven, Ceyran drank a glass of wine as he gazed at the empty vial on his desk. His mind was on the events that had transpired over the past few days.

Zaidera had been exporting crafts and food to the Kingdom of Salutania for a few years now. The same ship always carried the goods they sent, and Ceyran had been named its captain. The sea routes that connected Zaidera and the Kingdom of Salutania were relatively safe. He had crossed them many times now, and on this voyage, they had arrived in the Kingdom of Salutania without running into any more problems than usual.

Perhaps that was why he had been careless. An accident had occurred while they were unloading their cargo in their storeroom. By some error, a cargo tower collapsed, and the crew who had been handling the goods were pinned underneath.

The second he heard the collapse, Ceyran ran to check on his crew. Thankfully, no one had died, and there was minimal damage to the cargo itself. But just as he had feared, the people who were pinned beneath the collapse were injured, one of them gravely. Although every crew member was in theory replaceable, Ceyran's crew had been with him for many years now. A lesser man might have abandoned them or told them to seek treatment on their own, but Ceyran didn't have it in his heart to do so.

He ordered his crew to use all the potions they had to heal the injured, but one crew member was beyond help. This boy had been trapped beneath the heaviest crates, and his legs were in danger of needing to be amputated.

Ceyran's crew only carried low-grade HP potions, and these proved useless against such grievous injuries. If the injured crewman had been elderly, near retirement, Ceyran might have let it go. However, the victim was a boy in his teens. He was too young to be forced to live without his legs.

Moved by pity, Ceyran and his crew ran to every corner of Morgenhaven looking for potions. They tracked down the best alchemist in the city and purchased the strongest potion they could make. Even this had not been enough to heal the boy.

Ceyran knew Healing Magic could repair serious injuries that potions couldn't touch. However, he also knew that before long, neither magic nor potions would be able to heal the boy.

This understanding pushed Ceyran back into the city. He asked anyone he could find to direct him to a mage. Because of his urgency, he kept falling back into his native Zaideran, and people stared at him, uncomprehending.

Driven by fear, he found himself growing impatient—then a woman spoke out. A woman who wished to help him. She introduced herself as Sei, and she spoke Zaideran so fluently that for a moment, Ceyran saw the bright light of hope. However, in the next moment, it was extinguished.

There were no mages in Morgenhaven. Ceyran's shoulders dropped in resignation.

Then Sei gave him a potion. She seemed for all the world like an ordinary city girl handing over an ordinary potion that could be found anywhere. However, the liquid's color seemed the slightest bit darker than that of the low-grade HP potions with which Ceyran was familiar.

Maybe it's a mid-grade potion, he thought. He paused for a moment before saying, "Thank you."

His crew had already tried a mid-grade HP potion on their injured comrade. It hadn't done much. Maybe if they had two or three more, the boy might be able to move his legs once again, but a single potion likely wouldn't make a difference. Nevertheless, Ceyran took it, grateful for Sei's compassion.

After parting ways with Sei, he went to give the potion to the boy. Sei had given it to him for that purpose, after all.

The crew was astonished by the outcome: the boy's bones, which had been crushed by heavy crates, reknit into their natural shape, and within moments, he made a complete recovery.

As the crewmen cried out in joy, Ceyran picked up the empty potion vial and stared at it in shock. As he arrived at a conclusion, a chill ran down his spine. It was highly likely that Sei had given him a potion stronger than mid-grade—it had to be high-grade, nothing less. In Zaidera, high-grade potions could only be acquired by royalty, titled nobility, and other such powerful people.

Who in the world is Sei that she could so casually hand over something as valuable as this—and to a stranger, no less? Ceyran asked himself.

More importantly, he now had an even more critical concern. To receive something of such value and to pay nothing for it would be to shame the name of his country. He *owed* her.

Ceyran told his crew of the woman who had inadvertently saved their comrade, and they began their search at once. Fortunately, Ceyran found her without much trouble, and she accepted his efforts to repay her.

Now, Ceyran found himself staring at the empty vial of the potion Sei had given him. According to Oscar, Sei's father, who was the owner of a company or something like that, had commissioned the potion for Sei.

Just how large was Sei's family business? As the captain of a ship known for its foreign trade, Ceyran thought he knew all the major companies in the Kingdom of Salutania. One of the main merchant families had a daughter about Sei's age. Ceyran was acquainted with the patriarch, who was the chairman of a major company, as well as with the man's most powerful subordinates. He barely knew the fellow's daughter, though he was aware she was considered the heir to the company. He could recall no other young women in similar positions. He also remembered what the chairman looked like, but he didn't believe the man resembled Sei.

Maybe she was associated with a different company then?

In truth, Oscar had concealed Sei's identity most cleverly, and thus even as Ceyran tried to sort out Sei's connections, he remained at a loss. He still wanted to thank Sei's father. In addition, if possible, he wanted to learn the source of the high-grade potion.

Normally, Ceyran would have respected Sei's right to privacy, but the truth was that Ceyran's employer was searching for a uniquely talented alchemist. Ceyran didn't know the details of his employer's needs, but given the search, he thought it would be best to inform them of these events.

Those who could make high-grade potions were recognized as skilled alchemists in Zaidera as well. Ceyran knew with certainty that when he told his employer this tale, they would be dearly interested in the potion's provenance. Therefore, it was in his interest to gather as much information as he could in advance.

As the night wore on, Ceyran thought through all the things he needed to do before his ship departed for Zaidera.

However, Ceyran had misunderstood one key thing. His mistake was rooted in the fact that Sei had been wearing the clothes of a commoner despite apparently being the daughter of a wealthy merchant family.

In Zaidera, alchemists capable of making high-grade

potions could only be found in the imperial palace. As a result, only the emperor and powerful nobles could procure high-grade potions. However, in the Kingdom of Salutania, even commoners could *technically* obtain them if they tried hard enough.

Because of this difference, Ceyran assumed that people capable of making high-grade potions could be found in Salutanian towns. However, the truth was that, like in Zaidera, high-grade potions were only *truly* available to Salutania's royalty and high-ranking nobles. Not to mention, the potion that had cured his crewman had been made by the Saint. No one outside the palace would ever be able to obtain one of her potions. Ceyran had no way of knowing this, which made his information gathering rather difficult.

In the end, he was unable to ascertain any further information about the supposed alchemist or Sei's family company. Thus, a disappointed Ceyran left the Kingdom of Salutania.

◆ ◆ ◆

It was about time for the midday bell to ring when someone knocked on the door to the head researcher's office at the Research Institute of Medicinal Flora. Johan told them to come in, and the door opened to reveal Knight Commander Albert of the Knights of the Third Order.

"It's not often you stop by."

"I needed a break. And there's this." Albert held a document up to Johan, who looked at him with his eyes wide in surprise. Albert placed the document in Johan's outstretched hand.

As Johan shifted his gaze to the document, Albert took a seat on one of the sofas. Not long after, there was another knock at the door. Johan gave them permission to enter, and a servant did so, pushing a cart with a tea set on it.

"You asked for tea in advance?" asked Johan, looking surprised again.

"I happened to pass your attendant on the way, so I asked him to bring us some tea," Albert explained.

Johan chuckled, then signed the document before walking over to the sofa facing the one Albert was sitting in. The servant set a cup of tea in front of both men and then left the room at Johan's signal.

"So? What are you here for?" Johan asked.

"Nothing in particular. I just wanted to pass the time."

"Oh? Even though Sei's not here?" Johan grinned at Albert, who choked on his tea.

Albert glared at Johan as he stifled his laughter, but Johan blithely brushed off the look.

"Speaking of, how's the company doing?" Albert asked.

"Things have calmed down considerably. Thanks for asking."

"That's good then."

"Indeed. I thought things might get rough, since our sales would drop, but that doesn't seem to be the case."

"Because you let go of those cosmetics, you mean?"

"Precisely. In fact, letting those go ended up leading to an overall profit."

"The sabotage from your rivals was bad enough that this was the more desirable outcome, eh?"

"More or less."

Albert was also aware of the palace's efforts to put Sei in charge of her own company. As a knight commander, he was a member of the highest order of government. In addition, Sei was on the best of terms with the Third Order knights, and as a result, Albert always heard about anything related to her.

Albert also knew that House Valdec had been having a difficult time with their company. However, he couldn't thoughtlessly poke his nose into the problems of other houses. On top of that, he couldn't ask his own family—House Hawke—to intervene either, lest they kick up an even larger mess. The only thing he could do was listen to Johan's complaints and try to help him come up with a solution. The fact was that this helplessness frustrated him to no end. Therefore, Albert was relieved to hear that things had calmed down.

The palace had also had some concerns about Sei's company. Specifically, they had feared her old business partners wouldn't agree to relinquish the rights to her products. Sei's high-grade cosmetics were popular and profitable. It was easy to imagine that losing them as a source of income would be a blow for any business, no matter what else they might have for sale. The palace had been ready for a long negotiation at best and open resistance at worst. However, the company surprised everyone by throwing up their hands the first chance they got.

They gave in so easily in part because the palace offered to reimburse them for any outstanding investments. Between that and the promise of no longer having to deal with the underhanded tactics of rival companies, Sei's old business partners were relieved to let someone else take over.

However, they were further motivated by another, even more significant factor: the company understood that they owed a debt not only to the palace and House

Valdec but to the Saint for the profits they had enjoyed. You could say they had made this decision while thinking about their future relationships.

"Well, things may be better business-wise, but I bet things are going to get more trying for Sei from now on," Johan said.

"Why's that?"

"She's had to travel all over the kingdom to exterminate monsters, and she's now widely recognized. You know what's going to happen next, right?"

"You mean..."

"Having high social status means economic power. And she has a great deal of social clout. Plenty of men will set their sights on her."

Albert furrowed his brows, understanding all too well what Johan was getting at. He was talking about Sei getting married.

Marriageable age in the Kingdom of Salutania was younger than in Japan, so Johan and Albert were well within this bracket. For nobles, adulthood began at fifteen, and from then on they might get married at any time. As a result, it was typical for noblewomen to be married by twenty years of age.

That being said, Sei was considered rather old for an unmarried woman. However, as she was the Saint, had considerable income from her newly founded company, and was a fashionable trendsetter, no one saw her age as a problem. Even if she was a bit older than the average bride, her advantages more than made up for that. She was an incredibly attractive prospect, especially for sons who would not be named heir to their family.

Johan predicted that, in the near future, a deluge of portraits and personal statements would arrive at the palace, all addressed to Sei.

"Well, I doubt Sei's the type to consider marriage," Albert deflected. "She's already married to her work."

"That's true. I bet she'll either panic at the sight of the mountain of proposals or have the same look of distaste we're wearing right now."

"Ah... She's more likely to panic, isn't she?"

"Too true."

Sei was a late bloomer par excellence when it came to romance. As a result, she was incredibly slow at picking up on people's feelings for her. That much could be inferred based on how she hadn't even realized she had gone on a date with Albert until Johan pointed it out after the fact. Moreover, Sei didn't notice when men other than Albert made advances on her. The only people who did notice were those around her.

Both Johan and Albert knew Sei well. Therefore, they could easily imagine Sei blushing and becoming completely flustered by a flood of proposals. They burst out laughing at the thought.

"What about you?" Johan asked after a bit.

"Me?"

"You might be the son of a marquis, but if you take too long, someone might just steal her away from right under your nose."

"I know." Albert made a face. He didn't like having this pointed out.

It wasn't that Johan was trying to tease Albert, more that Johan was genuinely worried about his old friend. Albert understood this, which was why he bothered to reply, even though he made a face.

Albert knew his own feelings. He had only failed to make his intentions completely clear because he was trying to go at Sei's pace. She was a beginner when it came to romance. Albert's family seemed to have realized that, as they hadn't said a word about it.

However, Albert was probably going to have to take decisive action soon. Because Sei now controlled her own company, those who wished to take her profits for themselves would want to go after Sei herself. It went without saying that the quickest way to do this would be to marry Sei. Johan was right—it was clear that sooner or later, other houses would attempt to acquire the woman who was the Saint.

Albert really did have to summon his courage to make his move, and with all haste.

"If you don't pursue her," Johan mused, "then perhaps I will."

"What?!"

"I was just thinking I ought to offer myself as a prospective match before other weirdos try to claim the same."

Albert's face was fixed in a fearsome expression at his close friend's treacherous suggestion. Johan burst out laughing, and Albert slumped, drained of energy. What a terrible joke!

In truth, this was likely Johan's attempt to light a fire under his friend.

What transpired next was known only to them.

ACT 5
Debut

"A DEBUT?"

"That's right."

One day, while I was making potions like usual at the institute, Johan summoned me to his office to meet with an official from the palace. Johan and I sat down on one of the sofas as the official told us they would be holding a debut ceremony.

Whose debut? Mine, as it turned out.

It seemed a bit ridiculous to do this after I'd already been in the kingdom for so long, but when I considered the current state of affairs, I realized there was no avoiding it. Aira and I had been unexpectedly summoned to a world in crisis, threatened by miasma and monsters, so things had been a bit chaotic for the palace.

Thus, the Saint's debut had kept being postponed.

However, now that there weren't nearly so many monsters, it was finally time.

Honestly, I thought it would be better if everyone just let it go and didn't go out of their way to set anything up. When the king had formally apologized to me, there had been a sea of nobles present. Couldn't that count as my debut of sorts?

Welp, it didn't. That was just one of the little agonies that came with belonging to the upper echelons of society. I didn't really get *why* it wasn't okay, but everyone else seemed to have a ton of reasons for thinking so. For one thing, the apology hadn't been held in front of every single noble in the kingdom, so apparently everyone who'd missed the affair needed an invitation to the upcoming event.

"They'll hold your debut at the end of the season, then?" Johan asked while looking over the invitation addressed to him, which he had received from the official.

"Seems so. They'll be introducing me at a ball hosted by the royal family."

By "season," Johan was referring to the social season. During this period of time, most nobles left their domains to come to the capital, where they hosted and attended numerous parties and socialized with each other. No one was obligated to go to any particular event. However, the royal family hosted balls to mark the beginning and the end of the season, and if you received an invitation to either, you were expected to show up no matter what. Therefore, the officials at the palace figured that if my debut was held at one of these balls, nearly everyone would be able to attend.

My debut ceremony would be held in the afternoon, and the invitees included the heads of the families as well as anyone else who wished to observe. The evening ball was exclusive to adults, which was how it went every year.

That did mean there would be a social function not only in the evening but the afternoon as well. It seemed like it would be rather stressful for everyone involved, especially as the official assured me that everyone would go all out for the big day.

I also learned that a number of people had refrained from attending social events during the past season due to the threat of monster attacks. Some hadn't even come to the capital, being too busy contending with the monsters in their domains.

However, with the steep decline in the monster population, for the first time in a long while, the general outlook was cheerful. Having restrained themselves for so long, this year the nobility were sure to dress to the nines, especially since the end-of-season ball was to be even fancier than it had been lately.

"Don't just act like this is somebody else's problem," Johan said teasingly. "You have an obligation to attend both of these events."

My face fell. "I have to go to the ball too?"

Johan sighed. "Of course."

I would have gone happily if I could expect to be left alone as a wallflower. It would have been fun to see everyone dressed up in such a gorgeous setting. Unfortunately, since it would be right after my debut, people were going to go out of their way to pay extra attention to me. I had grown more accustomed to this, but I still hated being the center of attention.

Ah, well, no point wallowing in self-pity. I had to think positively. Johan had received an invitation as well, so at least one person I knew would be there. Would he be the only one...?

My face grew hot as I remembered something Albert had said to me before. I tried to cover it up, but in so doing, I gave myself away.

"What's wrong?" Johan asked.

"Nothing."

"All right, then."

Normally Johan would have pressed me for an answer, but for some reason, he didn't. I supposed the palace official was still there with us.

Does Albert actually remember asking to be my escort? Would he escort me to this ball? That would make me feel a lot *better about all this.*

The conversation with the official wrapped up as I was fretting, and we saw him off at the door to the institute.

The second he was gone, Johan turned to face me. "So? What was on your mind earlier?"

"Huh?"

"You were making a weird face."

"Oh..." I'd *just* managed to wipe the worry from my memory, but then he had to go and remind me. But the thought of bringing up the topic of my escort was too flustering to articulate, so I changed the subject. "I'm just a little bit worried about the ball."

"Why?"

"I bet I'll be the main event."

"Of course you will be."

"Right." I sighed heavily.

"Do you dislike the notion so very much?"

"I'm just not comfortable with it. I'd prefer to hang out around the edge."

"Not a chance."

"I had a feeling." I understood that, but I deflated all over again when he said it.

Seeing me so disheartened made Johan chuckle. "I did

just receive this invitation, so don't worry. I'll be with you."

"Thank you."

"I bet Al will be there as well. He'll be a better shield than I will, I suspect."

My heart skipped a beat at that name. I dropped my gaze to the ground so that Johan didn't notice. "Lord Hawke will be there too?"

"I'm sure of it. He's the knight commander of the Knights of the Third Order, after all. There's no way he won't be invited."

"I suppose that's true."

"In fact, I'm sure he'll be overjoyed to have a chance to request your permission to escort you."

This time I heard the laughter in his voice and looked up to find him grinning. I pouted to hide the fact that my cheeks were burning, which made Johan's laughter escape him.

A few days later, just as Johan predicted—or had he known something I hadn't?—Albert asked to be my escort.

"So, about that ball after your debut..."

"Yes?"

I had gone to Albert's office to deliver a document

regarding potions the Order had ordered when he suddenly stopped me from leaving with those words. I balked and turned to find him blushing ever so slightly.

Such destructive power! Even I started to blush.

"Would you like me to be your escort?" he asked.

"Um, yes...please..." We had discussed this before, during one of my dance lessons. Did he remember that? I trailed off at the end there, but my answer made him smile happily.

For some reason, the temperature in the room suddenly shot up.

"Shall I come fetch you at your chambers in the palace?"

"Y-yeah. I'll be there all day."

Both my debut and the ball would be held on palace grounds. It would take even more time for me to get ready than it did for my lessons, so I was going to be sleeping at the palace the night before.

I had seen my maids just a day ago, and they were already in incredibly high spirits about the whole ordeal. They were planning to give me a massage before I went to sleep and to be even more attentive the morning of. One had clenched her fist as she declared this would be a grand test of their power.

I'll tell you a secret—the fervor in their eyes scared me a bit.

I was to wear a different dress for each event. This was one reason for my maids' enthusiasm. I would need to change clothes between the debut and the ball, which meant I wouldn't get a break. However, I couldn't complain. My attendants would be the ones doing all the hard work—all I had to do was sit there.

"My maids are really excited about my costume change." I felt kinda self-conscious, so I looked sideways as I told Albert about all this.

"Is that so?"

"Mm-hmm. So, yeah, that's why I'm going to be staying at the palace the night before."

Because I wasn't looking at him, my heartbeat gradually slowed. However, I probably shouldn't have looked away. I wound up missing Albert's mischievous expression—he'd just thought of something.

I heard the scraping of his chair and looked back up again to find he had walked right over to me. Just as I frowned in confusion, he lifted a lock of my hair and brought it to his lips.

"I can't wait to see you all dressed up," he said with a chuckle as he kissed my hair.

I gasped, and my once-wrangled heart ran wild again.

Time passed in the blink of an eye, and the day of my debut finally arrived. My skin was all shiny and supple thanks to my overnight spa experience in my chambers at the palace. I was surprised. The difference in my skin was immediately clear as soon as the maids finished my massage. It was as if I had been reborn. I couldn't hide my even greater surprise upon waking the next morning—my skin was still perfectly smooth and glowing.

"Is something the matter?"

"No, I'm just surprised that my skin looks as good as it did yesterday."

"Well, we did use your skincare cream, my lady."

"Oh, that can't be it. I think it's because you're all such skilled masseuses. Thank you."

"You flatter us, my lady."

They truly were good with their hands. I doubted I could develop a product that would do half of what their skills accomplished. Mary and my other maids grinned with delight as I once again expressed my gratitude.

After my makeup was finished, it was time to get dressed. One of my maids brought out a robe just like she had for my Lady's Days and showed it to me. "This is what you shall be wearing for your debut ceremony."

"This?"

I'd thought I'd be in the same robe I had worn during my formal audience with the king, but this one was, er, different. It had the same aesthetic—white cloth with golden embroidery—but it was even more ornate. To begin with, far more of the fabric had been embroidered, and the designs even more intricate. Clear gems had been threaded through the patterns, and they glittered in the light.

It was so magnificent that I couldn't help but stare at it, dumbfounded. Words of protest threatened to pour out of my mouth, but I held them in. I had a feeling that if I declined this option, my only other options were even fancier.

My maids clearly guessed what I was thinking, because to a one, they wore placating smiles.

"You look lovely."

"Th-thank you."

With that, Saint Version 2.0 was complete. I worried I looked ridiculous, but my maids beamed as they nodded, and every last one of them had something nice to say, so it had to be okay, right?

I honestly felt like the robe was wearing *me*, but I also felt like that thought didn't give enough credit to the maids who'd worked so hard to make me presentable in it, so I pushed it down.

Now that I was ready, all I could do was wait while sipping the tea Mary had made for me. Before long, there was a knock at the door. My escort had arrived.

My escort for this event was a knight I didn't recognize. He was probably from the First or Second Order, though. We exchanged rote greetings and headed to the venue.

One knight stood ahead of me, one to my left, one to my right, and yet another behind. I was surrounded by them as we walked down the corridors of the palace. Talk about pretentious. I knew there was nothing I could do about it because of decorum, but it was so over-the-top that my smile turned stiff.

Nevertheless, my lessons had taught me that when out in public, the Saint—or rather, a noble lady—always slightly curved up the corners of her mouth so that she wore an eternally gentle expression. I tried to do as much while we walked through the palace, but if my teacher had seen the rigid expression I kept falling back into, I would have received a failing grade.

After a few minutes, we arrived at the entry hall where those who would participate in the ceremony had gathered. At the head of the group, I spotted the king and the prime minister. They said something to a knight standing nearby before turning to face me. The ring of people parted, opening a path for me to make my way to the two of them.

One of the knights led me over. I was so nervous under the stares of even this group that I couldn't think of anything to say beyond, "Thank you for arranging everything for today." I figured that would be harmless enough. Hopefully.

The king smiled—point to Sei, she passed the test! "It was our pleasure," he said. "I am even more pleased to at last formally welcome you into society."

Greetings done with, it was time to begin. Everyone who had a role to play had now arrived. The king moved to stand in front of the grand doors to the main hall, and I went to stand behind him. A servant opened the doors, and the murmurs we heard coming from the other side fell silent.

The tall king was like a wall, so I couldn't see past him, but I knew there were a lot, a lot, *a lot* of people present, and my nerves started getting the best of me.

Keep calm. Get a hold of yourself. I took several deep breaths.

The king began to walk. I stared at his back so I wouldn't look at anyone else as I entered the hall. We soon turned and headed up the stairs of a tall platform. The king stopped in the middle and faced the front of the crowd. I stopped a few steps behind and to his left, where I did the same. We had rehearsed this bit before.

Thank goodness for that. I had been taught where to stand and what to do in advance. I probably would have just flailed about in confusion otherwise. I was profoundly grateful to the officials who had taken the time to walk me through it all, despite how busy they had been with everything else they'd had to do to throw this event together. It was thanks to them that I was able to stand on that stage without losing my mind.

"The Saint was brought to us thanks to the Saint Summoning Ritual, and today, I present her to you."

Upon hearing the king's words, I pinched my robe to lift the skirt and perform a curtsy. I dropped my gaze to my feet as I did so, but I sensed everyone bowing or curtsying back to me.

As I straightened, I looked ahead and saw that sea of eyes turned on me. I froze. I was so nervous that I wanted to throw up. I had to do something or I would stare blankly into space forever.

The king continued next to me, speaking of monsters and of my efforts to slay them in the countryside, which had already seen the results of my actions. Some people knew this story already, but in this speech, the king officially made the news that monsters were no longer a threat common knowledge. The atmosphere brightened at this. However, I didn't notice. I was still staring straight ahead, sliding into panic.

Then I spotted Johan, standing in the back. He was dressed formally in an elaborately decorated knee-length coat and vest. *I've never seen him all fancied up like this before,* I thought.

Our eyes met. Johan lifted an eyebrow and grinned as he pointed somewhere close to the platform. I followed his pointing and my eyes landed on Albert.

Albert wore his knightly regalia, and he had been watching the king with an impassive expression, but when he noticed my gaze, his face softened. Just a little.

My body instantly relaxed, and an answering smile spread across my face. That one glimpse brought me so much comfort, and I managed to raise my eyes enough to see that Albert was accompanied by some other familiar faces.

Yuri and Lord Smarty-Glasses were wearing much showier robes than usual. Yuri noticed my attention and gave a small wave. Lord Smarty-Glasses, standing behind him, just furrowed his brows ever so magnificently. That turned my smile into a chuckle.

What the heck are you doing, Grand Magus?

Amused by Yuri's typical lack of decorum, I glanced

around again. This time, I spotted someone I wasn't expecting: Liz.

Huh? What's she doing here? My eyes widened in surprise. Liz saw me notice her, and the smile on her face deepened. I smiled more broadly in turn. *I really thought there'd only be adults at this thing, but I guess not.*

As I looked closer at the crowd, I spotted other people about Liz's age.

Now that I think about it, the ball is supposed to be adults only—but I didn't hear anything about an age restriction for this event. That must be it.

Soon, the king finished his speech and concluded the ceremony. I followed him back out of the hall.

"You did well in there," the king said as I sighed with relief.

"Thank you."

"You must be tired. You ought to go rest in your chambers until the ball."

"Thank you. I shall do just that."

"Then we shall see you tonight."

While I was okay physically, it was true that I was mentally exhausted—even though the whole thing hadn't even lasted that long! The king clearly understood how I was feeling, so he didn't drag out our conversation any longer.

I heard increasingly loud noises coming from the hall where the people were still milling, but I opted to take the king up on his offer and headed back to my chambers. I asked the knight who had been my guide to escort me back. I didn't want to impose, but I also didn't know the layout of this part of the palace. I doubted I could make my way back on my own.

The knight readily accepted and escorted me with the same squad of knights as before.

"I'm back."

"Welcome back." Mary greeted me with a smile.

She led me over to the sofa, and one of my other maids brought some tea. Had they been told in advance that I was coming? They seemed awfully prepared.

As I relaxed with my tea, one of my maids standing closer to the door began to move as if she had noticed something. Was someone here? I watched curiously as she spoke with someone outside the door before coming over to me.

"I apologize for disturbing you while you're at rest, but you have guests."

"I do? Who?"

"His Royal Highness Prince Rayne and Lady Ashley."

I was surprised to hear this, to say the least. Liz was one thing, but Prince Rayne? It seemed rude to leave them waiting out in the hallway, so I told her to bring them in at once.

I stood, and Liz and I curtsied to one another. We were both being more formal than usual because of the other guest.

"Good afternoon, Sei."

"And a good afternoon to you as well, Liz."

"I apologize for intruding during your private time, but I simply had to see you in that gorgeous robe up close."

"Is that so? Well, please don't concern yourself with me. And may I ask who is accompanying you today?" It would be best to get this part out of the way sooner rather than later.

"This is your first time meeting him, isn't it? Allow me to introduce you to the second prince of our kingdom."

Hearing it from the maid was one thing, but hearing it from Liz herself was something else. Here he was, the second prince. He had the same red hair and red eyes as the king, though his looks were a bit softer than his father's. Maybe he took after his mother.

"I apologize for not introducing myself sooner. I am Rayne Salutania. It is my utmost honor to make your acquaintance, Lady Saint."

I was taken aback by his exceptionally polite manner. "The honor is all mine, Your Highness. My name is Sei

Takanashi. Please, there's no need to be so formal with me. I am not used to speaking so."

It was thanks to my etiquette instructor that I didn't squeak in some unseemly way—and also that I was able to keep my composure.

"Very well, then. I shall do as you request."

Greetings accomplished, I invited them to sit on the sofas. Liz and I took one while Prince Rayne sat across from us. A maid handed us fresh cups of tea as we did so.

"I apologize for intruding during your rest," Prince Rayne said with a cheerful smile.

"It's quite all right."

"I've heard so much about you from Lady Ashley, so I wanted very much to meet you."

Liz had been planning to come see me after the event, and when the prince had heard, he had asked to come along. It sounded like Liz had really talked me up, so I feared His Highness thought I was, shall we say, kinda cool. Prince Rayne told me shyly that he had wanted to meet someone of such astounding virtue.

What the heck has Liz been saying about me?! I had every reason to be wailing internally. I mean, I didn't deserve such praise! I wasn't virtuous or saintly in any regard at all!

"I see," I said as I trembled under the weight of the prince's expectations.

His expression suddenly grew serious. "Please, Lady Saint, you must also allow me to apologize for my elder brother's actions. He caused you such offense."

"Your elder brother? Oh, right..." For a moment, I didn't follow, but then it hit me. He was referring to the crown prince. I had completely forgotten about that kid. "The king has already formally apologized on his behalf. Please, don't worry yourself about it as well, Your Highness."

"I thank you for your magnanimity."

"Don't, uh, I mean, you are welcome."

He'd gotten all formal again, which flustered me.

Prince Rayne smiled ruefully and quietly apologized again.

Honestly, I had considered the whole thing over and done with after the king's formal apology, but the prince seemed to have been fretting about it for a while.

He sure has a strong sense of duty.

I didn't know what to do with someone blameless trying to take responsibility for something, so I just accepted the apology for now. I really hoped he wouldn't let it bother him anymore, especially since I myself had already forgotten it.

With that over, Liz started speaking in a cheerful voice to help lighten the mood. "It's my turn now."

"What do you mean?"

"I was the one who wanted to talk to you first. His Highness merely tagged along without my permission," Liz said primly, which made the prince chuckle.

Liz was being a bit more forward than usual, which I suspected she was doing on purpose to cheer us up. Plus, the prince's reactions made me pretty sure that these two were close friends.

"I have to say, I was surprised to see you at the debut," I said.

"We aren't allowed at the evening ball, but I simply couldn't afford to miss the opportunity to see you in all your finery. So, I asked my father to permit me to attend."

"I usually dress up for our tea parties. I would hardly count this a special occasion."

"But you usually wear *gowns* during the tea parties, and now you're wearing that splendid robe."

"True..."

"And I'm sure you'll be wearing a far more gorgeous gown for the ball than you do for our little get-togethers. I would so like to see how you look in that as well."

Ack, it was so *cute* how Liz sounded like she was sulking. I couldn't help but want to indulge her.

In the end, we agreed to go to more parties together next year, since she'd be considered an adult by then.

I dreaded standing out, but Liz seemed pleased, and that was good enough for me. My maids seemed pretty pleased with this promise as well.

After that, the three of us chatted for a bit about their lives at the Royal Academy, and before I knew it, it was time to get ready for the ball.

It was so fun chatting with them; I really got absorbed in the conversation. The three of us promised to have tea again sometime soon, and with that, our impromptu tea party came to an end.

The curtain of night began to fall, and my escort arrived at my chambers. I fluttered with anxiety as I stood from the sofa and looked toward the door. Albert stepped into the room and stopped, his eyes widened just so.

"I look forward to this evening," I said.

"Me...me too..." Despite my greeting, Albert seemed at a loss for words. He continued to stare. At me.

I knew it! This dress was *totally* wearing me. Oof. I didn't bother asking how I looked.

The gown was even more extravagant than the kind I usually got stuffed into. It was adorned with jewels that glimmered in the light every time I moved. The jewels alone made it luxurious, but the dress was made out of some kind of heavy white cloth that shimmered with a golden sheen. It was embroidered with the same kinds of designs as the robe I had worn that afternoon. Additionally, multiple layers of sheer lace and golden stumpwork embroidery covered my chest and elbows; three-dimensional ribbons, flowers, and other designs accentuated the gown here and there.

In brief, I had zero confidence that I looked like the kind of person who should be wearing this unquestionably exquisite dress. My maids claimed that I looked stunning, and I didn't like to gainsay them. However, as a commoner, I just didn't have the self-assurance required to pull it off.

Meanwhile, Albert looked just as I expected him to. Instead of his usual uniform, he wore finery more appropriate for a ball, and he looked terribly dashing. His coat was made of a lustrous dark blue cloth. Intricate golden embroidery ran along the edges of his lapel, placket, and hem. The vest he wore underneath was white and embroidered all over with colorful flowers.

Although he looked far more dapper than he normally did, unlike me, he was the sort of person who looked oh-so-natural in these kinds of clothes. Must have been because he really was from a noble family.

I was captivated by the sight of him, I admit—so much so that I frankly deserved a little praise for managing to actually speak first.

We continued silently taking one another in until Albert broke the silence. "I apologize. You look so pretty that I couldn't find the words."

"H-huh?"

Now it was my turn to be at a loss. That had made a real impact on me. He had complimented me before, the few times he had seen me wearing a gown, but today his offensive prowess was truly something.

It's like he's three times more powerful than usual because he's dressed up all nice like that. Despite this thought, I couldn't tamp down the bashfulness, and my cheeks grew hot. I tried to think of something to say, something that would hide my shyness, but instead I accidentally blurted, "You also look..."

"Hm?"

"Oh! Uh! Never mind!"

Calm down, me! What was I on the verge of saying?! I realized mid-sentence how embarrassing I was about to be and fell straight into panic. However, my attempt to cover up my own self-consciousness didn't work at all, because now Albert was blushing too. *What am I supposed to do in this kind of situation?!*

We both sank into silence again, which was interrupted by the sound of someone clearing their throat. It was the official who had come with Albert. "It is almost time for the ball."

I snapped back to my senses. My maids were all smiling at me.

Oh, nooo! I've done it again... I mentally cringed. *Here lies Sei, doomed to repeat history.*

"Oh! Sorry!" I felt on the verge of tears as I apologized to the official, who looked awfully awkward.

At last, we started making our way to the ball.

The ball was being held in a different hall from where I'd had my debut. It was the biggest room in the palace. The doors were proportionate to the room's grandeur—as big as the doors I'd had to pass through for my audience with the king. I looked up at them from where we stood at the back of the line of people waiting to go inside.

The people with the lowest court rank entered first, and those with higher ranks followed behind. As the Saint, that made me last, with the exception of the king, who was hosting the ball. By the time we reached the door, nearly everyone had already gone inside.

The moment someone went in, a footman announced their name for the guests already inside. In a way, I was just another person who had been invited to the ball, but all eyes were sure to be on me. I cowered at the thought.

"Feeling nervous?" Albert asked, concern in his tone. I had tensed up.

"Yeah."

Albert rubbed the back of the hand I had wrapped around his arm to soothe me. I looked up at him to find him looking back at me with a gentle smile. I relaxed a bit. It was almost as if he had told me not to worry.

That's right. I've got him by my side now. I won't be on my own, like I was at the debut. The warmth on my hand gave me courage to proceed through the doors.

"Lord Albert Hawke, son of Marquis Hawke, and Lady Sei Takanashi." Our names were announced as we entered the ballroom. As expected, everyone turned toward us.

I tried to smile like I had been taught to in class, but I feared that my expression looked too forced. I focused on the throne in the back of the room, ignored everyone else around me, and somehow managed to overcome my anxiety.

I let Albert guide me toward the throne and successfully avoided bumping into anyone along the way. Maybe it was my Saint's power at work. I kind of felt like Moses parting the Red Sea.

I stared straight ahead as we proceeded to the throne.

We stopped in front of it, and it wasn't long before the king entered the ballroom from a door nearer to the dais.

He paused to give a speech, which formally started the ball. He reminded us of the greatly diminished number of monsters, which inspired cheer in the gathered crowd. However, it didn't improve my mood all that much.

As I thought about what would come next, I was once again seized with apprehension.

Though the speech was made by a man of great power, he kept it short. The king raised his right hand, and the orchestra that had been on standby began to play music. It was finally time.

Albert led me to the center of the ballroom. Once we arrived at our designated spot, I let go of Albert's arm, and we turned to face one another. I returned his bow with a curtsy. We began to dance.

I moved my body to the music as I strove to remember the right steps. Even though I was panicking in my mind, I took care to smile and try to appear graceful.

As we danced, Albert spoke. "Sei."

"Yes?"

"Look at me?"

Oh, right! I was supposed to look at my dance partner's face. My head had been fixed staring straight ahead, so I turned my face to him. He smiled sweetly at me.

His passionate gaze scored a direct hit. I missed a step, but Albert quickly righted me.

This is taking all I've got. Please don't attack me like that right now!

"Sorry," I apologized.

"No, that was my fault. I did it without thinking. You're so tense."

Feeling guilty about the crime you committed, eh? I shot him an accusing look, and he apologized again. But why was he smiling while he did so? Maybe it was because we were dancing, but he seemed too amused for that. I couldn't help but feel like he'd done it more to tease me than to help me relax. It was fair to be a bit miffed, right?

During this exchange, the dance neared the final stage.

Phew. I think I'll be able to make it all the way through.

"Sei...I'm glad we could dance together. Thank you."

"Thank you as well. It was fun," I responded with a smile just as the dance came to an end.

At that, Albert bowed, and I curtsied again. All around us, the people clapped.

◆◆◆

After that arduous trial, Albert led me over to the wall. The people we passed were going to be dancing during the next song. This was a ball, after all, and there would be many more songs and many more dances.

I saw Johan waiting where we were headed. I didn't recognize him at first, as he was dressed up for the ball too. I was struck. He really was handsome, wasn't he?

Johan took a couple of glasses from a page walking by and held them out to us. "Nice dancing out there."

"Thanks."

"Thank you."

I casually took a sip of the drink. I thought it would be alcohol, but it turned out to be fruity water. I was quite thirsty after all that dancing, so I appreciated Johan's forethought.

"Looks like they've been teaching you well, here at the palace. You're an excellent dancer now."

"You think so? I tried really hard not to mess up any of the steps."

"I mean it, you did wonderfully. You did have Al to help if you made any mistakes, so it's not like you would've had any problems anyway."

"It certainly didn't feel that way in the moment! What with everyone staring at me."

Johan hadn't been the one out there dancing under so much scrutiny, so I wished he would stop making it sound like it had been so easy.

Albert seemed to feel the same way. "If that's so, then maybe you should get out on the dance floor too."

"Oh, don't suggest something so absurd. You know I've distanced myself from all this."

"But you *have* to dance with Sei, or—" Albert lowered his voice a bit, then stopped and took a sip from his glass before silently averting his gaze.

Johan glanced around as well and heaved a sigh. "Well, I suppose I am here because I was worried this would happen."

"It's just as you predicted," Albert agreed.

They looked exhausted, but they seemed to be discussing something I wasn't privy to.

What are they talking about? I peered about curiously, but something stopped me.

Johan cleared his throat and schooled his countenance. "May I have this dance, my lady?"

I was speechless. He had spoken in such a perfectly formal manner. As I blinked at his fake smile, I thought absentmindedly that, until now, I had never really gotten the impression that he truly was a noble.

I couldn't stop staring at him in surprise. He kept his expression utterly serene as he whispered, "Answer me."

I swiftly placed my hand in his proffered palm, and he guided my fingers to his arm. "Johan?"

"You can look around but only with your eyes. Don't move your head. You'll see those who have set their sights on you."

"Huh? What do you mean?"

That had an awfully dangerous sound to it. I cautiously cast my eyes about the room and noticed, here and there, people who were watching me.

Johan explained in subdued tones that these were people who wished to become "acquainted" with me. They were watching me like predators on the hunt, hungry for an opportunity to pounce. The fastest man to "make my acquaintance" would have the privilege of inviting me to dance.

"You'd rather dance with me than with someone you don't know, right?" Johan asked.

"You're absolutely right about that." I was uncomfortable enough dancing with Johan, but doing the same with a stranger was far too high a hurdle for me.

However, while I didn't mind dancing with him, I had never done so before. I was fairly sure that I was about to trample his feet.

If I do, I suppose I'll give him a potion. A low-grade HP one would work, right? I thought as the song came to an end, and the people intending to dance next proceeded to the center of the hall.

As we walked, I apologized in advance, just in case I actually did step on his foot.

"By the way, *can* you dance?" I asked.

"Good question. It's been a long time since I last came to a ball. I have little confidence in my skills."

"Oh. Well, if I do trip all over you, shall I grace you with a potion?"

"I wouldn't use something so important for that. Just try not to break my toes," he chuckled as the dance began.

I was pretty sure Johan was lying when he claimed to have low confidence in his skills. Dancing with him felt different from dancing with Albert, but Johan was a good lead, and he made it easy. I talked to him every day, so I didn't feel weirdly nervous or anything. I actually suspected that I danced even better than I had before. It might just have been my imagination, though.

"What should I do after this dance?" I asked. I thankfully felt comfortable enough to hold a conversation. "Shall I keep alternating between you and Lord Hawke as my partner?"

I was really hoping I could get away with giving my favor to the two of them all night, but Johan crushed those hopes.

"Al might want to keep going, but I'm done after this."

"But I can just stay with Lord Hawke for the rest of the night, right?"

"You can, but I think Al is looking for reinforcements even as we speak."

"Oh! Is he?"

"Indeed, I saw him wander off just a moment ago."

I understood the need to find alternates. I had learned in my etiquette classes that dancing with the same person over and over was considered problematic in a number of ways. Thankfully, Albert was trying to ensure that I wouldn't have to dance with strangers. But who in the world could act as such a reinforcement? Other knights from the Third Order?

I recalled the faces of the knights I knew as the song came to an end and we headed back to our original location. There was indeed someone I recognized waiting for us—someone I had not expected.

"Good evening, Lady Sei."

"Good evening, Lord Drewes."

Yuri was the last person I had imagined filling in for Albert. And standing behind him was Lord Smarty-Glasses.

"We heard you were in need of our aid, so here we are," Yuri said with a radiant smile. He was also dressed in ballroom attire, looking as beautiful as you'd imagine a prince should look.

"Oh, thank you very much."

I was genuinely surprised to see Yuri here. He was never interested in anything other than magic. Was he just used to participating in these kinds of things as the head of the Royal Magi Assembly?

Not so much, it turned out. According to Lord Smarty-Glasses, it was unusual for Yuri to show his face even at the end-of-season ball. I looked at Lord Smarty-Glasses curiously, and he simply said: "His older brother ordered him to come."

Older brother? Huh? Yuri has an older brother? My mind was full of question marks, but the next song was beginning, so I went back out to the dance floor with Yuri.

Much to my surprise, Yuri knew how to dance as well. He had good reflexes to boot, as might be expected from someone known to be obsessed with fighting. However, his personality came out in the way he led—he was much more forceful than Albert and Johan had been.

It really was a different experience, dancing with different partners. I'd just learned something new. I had only ever really danced with my teacher before.

After Yuri, I did a round with Lord Smarty-Glasses. I was told later that it was unusual for Lord Smarty-Glasses to dance as well, so there was some commotion as we made our way to the dance floor. There had been a bit of murmuring when Yuri accompanied me, but people hadn't gasped about it as much as they were now. It really was a rare show.

Incidentally, in terms of who was best at leading, I would rank Lord Smarty-Glasses just after Albert.

I learned later from Johan that he and the other three were notorious no-shows at the balls. It was no wonder then that I had received some rather frightening looks. I really wished they had warned me about that first! Being glared at like that without knowing why had done horrors to my stomach. I really would have appreciated being prepared for that ahead of time...

In any case, thanks to the four of them, I managed to survive the grand affair.

◆ ◆ ◆

After my debut into society, my halcyon days of nothing-much returned. I had feared that once my existence became public knowledge, nobles I had never met before would try to make my acquaintance, but they largely left me alone.

"It sure is peaceful," I murmured as I handed Johan a cup of coffee in his office.

Johan took the cup and savored its aroma as he looked up at me. "Why do you say that?"

"Well, everything's gone back to the way it was before my debut."

"Ah. Well, the palace is probably working to ensure that."

"They are?" I tilted my head to the side inquisitively, prompting Johan to provide more details.

Thanks to his and Albert's efforts to guard me during the ball, no one had been able to get close to me. However, that didn't mean that every interested person had given up. Those who were still fixated on forging a connection with me were probably sending invitations to tea parties and balls to the palace in an effort to somehow make my acquaintance.

"I haven't received any invitations, though."

"I expect the palace officials are politely declining them."

"You think so?"

"There are still monsters out there, right? I imagine they're using that as the excuse."

We hadn't received any news about another black swamp yet. However, I was on standby so that I could be deployed as soon as they found one. And of course, monster slaying took precedence over tea parties and the like, so I understood how that made for a good excuse when it came to social events.

"In that case, I can just focus on my research for the time being."

"Hah! That's right."

But wouldn't you know it, I jinxed myself that day, laughing and chatting with Johan. My plan was immediately foiled.

Just as I was about to leave Johan's office, there was a knock at the door. Johan invited them in, and a servant entered along with one of the palace officials. The grave expression on the official's face made clear that I was about to be asked to go to the palace with all possible speed.

Bonus Story 1

ONE MORNING, the mood in the institute's kitchen was far more cheerful than usual, on account of the fact that we had a guest. A *lady* guest.

The cheerful voices of my male colleagues filled the kitchen. Aira had come to visit.

"Good morning, Sei! Thanks for having me today."

"Morning, Aira. Thanks for coming."

Aira showed up a bit after we had finished eating breakfast. We had promised each other that we would get around to baking together. We both had a day off, so we were finally fulfilling that promise.

We went to the kitchen and Aira greeted the chefs. They beamed at her. It felt like everyone was wearing far sunnier smiles than usual. I guess that's just the power of an adorable young lady.

Well, I couldn't say that I didn't understand. Although Aira was just wearing comfortable clothes that were easy to move in, it being her day off, her daisy-yellow dress looked cute as heck on her. She was especially darling when she tied that white apron over it.

While the chefs cleaned up breakfast and started getting things ready for lunch, they directed Aira to a corner of the kitchen. I had collected all of the ingredients we were going to use and laid them out on the counter, so we were ready to start measuring.

"Did you make this a lot back in Japan?" Aira asked me.

"Yup, especially when I was still in school."

"But not after you graduated?"

"Nope. I was so busy with work, I never had the energy."

To be more accurate, I was so busy that I'd never had the *time*, but I bet I would've if I had. I might have even made udon and bread from scratch. Kneading dough did strike me as good stress relief.

"But you did make it a lot a long time ago, then?"

"Well, not really, just once in a while."

"Huh? I'm surprised you can remember the measurements, in that case," Aira said with a look of wide-eyed wonder, making me blush. Something like that wasn't really worth praising!

"It's not that complicated," I protested.

It really was easy as anything to remember the basic ingredients and quantities for pound cake. That was what was on the menu today, and true to its name, pound cake required exactly the same amount of its four ingredients: flour, butter, sugar, and eggs. It was so easy to remember that I'd never been able to forget it after the first time I stumbled upon the recipe.

Granted, having now made pound cake several times since my summoning, I had made some slight adjustments to the measurements. Cookies used the same basic ingredients and in similar ratios, but they required twice as much flour as the other ingredients. With that alternative ratio in mind, it had been relatively easy to start iterating on the combination.

For example, when I added dried fruit, I used the basic recipe as a foundation and then experimented.

Aira praised me yet again when I told her this. Too much!

"I'm surprised it takes so *much* of these ingredients to make a cake, though," she said.

"The volume of butter and sugar is especially surprising, isn't it?"

"Yeah! So how much do we need to measure out?"

"We're going to be making a large batch today, so..."

Aira was shocked when I told her the full amount.

However, we were making half again as many cakes as I usually did. It had been a while since the last time I made them, as I had been busy on expeditions. I was planning to divvy the cakes between Johan, Jude, and the other researchers. Of course, I also intended to give Aira some to take back with her.

Aira smiled happily at this promise. "Your cakes are hugely popular among the mages too, you know."

"Really?"

"Yup."

I had given Aira cakes multiple times now. She said she ate them during her breaks at work and shared them with her colleagues when they took breaks at the same time. The first people she had let try my cakes had said they were gentle on the tongue and the stomach, as they weren't overly sugary. From there, the word had spread. A whole bushel of people were looking forward to their share of this batch.

In that case, I should probably give Aira more than I was planning to. If I don't, she won't have much to eat herself.

We poured the pound cake batter into molds, then rolled the cookie dough into cylinders, which we cut into slices. After we placed the cookies on a baking tray, Aira started peering around the kitchen. "Where's the oven?"

"Over there."

"This? Huh? You use firewood?!" Aira was bewildered to learn that we needed firewood to heat our oven.

"Never fear."

"Oh, wow!"

We had veteran chefs on hand. One of them came over with a smile and took the tray from Aira.

"Thank you."

The chef returned her thanks with a smile. "Don't mention it."

This exchange was quite familiar to me. To tell you the truth, I still couldn't control the temperature of the flames on my own yet. I therefore often relied on the chefs to handle it for me. They were always helping me out, so in turn, I always made sure to give them some of whatever I had concocted on a given day. Of course, I planned to give them a share today as well.

"It'll be a while before everything's done baking, so how about we have some tea?"

"Good idea!" Aira beamed.

I got some hot water from a chef, made herbal tea for the two of us, and we headed into the dining hall. This time, I chose chamomile tea. It was a mild, soothing drink, and I had unintentionally favored it lately.

"Making cakes and cookies sure takes a lot of hard work."

"You can say that again. It's even harder in this world because we don't have all those nifty gadgets we had back in Japan." I nodded with Aira as I rubbed my upper arm.

Granted, making cakes and cookies had been rough going even with the advanced baking tools of modern Japan. It went without saying that it was profoundly more difficult without those tools.

With pound cakes, the more batter you wanted to work with, the more oomph you had to put into mixing. If not for my Healing Magic, I'd have been sore from shoulder to fingertip the next morning. To prevent that, I used magic on myself starting from right that moment. I was pretty sure that I was the only person I knew who would use magic for this sort of thing, though.

Aira was surprised when she saw me Heal myself, but of course she would have been. Who would expect some-one to use magic to buff up their body just to bake?

Speaking of, the chefs never relied on their magic when they cooked. They relied purely on the strength of their own muscles when we baked together. It was important for them to hone their stamina so they could cook at their best even when they didn't have a mage with reinvigorating magic to rely on. The chefs were far superior to me in that regard.

"I think if you taught me the recipe, I might be able to do the prep work myself, but I doubt I'd be able to handle the baking part on my own," Aira said.

"I always have the chefs help me out. Were you hoping to make these on your own later?"

"Mm-hmm. I always get flustered asking others for help. But, well, I don't have anywhere to bake anyway, so it's not like I could really do that."

"Ah, yeah."

A place to cook, huh? It made me think. A certain kind of Water Magic enchantment could turn an item into a water supply of sorts. Aira could use Water Magic herself, so she would have that covered so long as she had a basin to act as a sink. What about a stove? Was it possible to make a stovetop with a Fire Magic enchantment? If it was, then I bet Aira could have a tiny kitchen just about anywhere in the Assembly barracks.

"Have you thought of maybe getting a slab enchanted with Fire Magic so it could be a kind of stove?"

"Oh! We actually have something like that! Though it's only really for heating water." According to Aira, it didn't even bring the water to boiling—just warmed it up a bit.

Is there a way to make it a bit stronger? I thought.

But just then, a wondrous fragrance came wafting

out of the kitchen. Our cakes and cookies would be ready soon. We paused our conversation and practically skipped into the kitchen.

◆ ◆ ◆

I walked down the hall to the office of the knight commander of the Knights of the Third Order. I was carrying the goodies I had made with Aira.

Albert doesn't like overly sugary desserts, but these are simple and I just used the basic recipe, so it should be okay, I'd thought as I set aside his portion earlier.

To tell you the truth, I had no choice but to give Albert a share. I'd stopped giving him homemade desserts for a time because I had found out he didn't care for sugary snacks. But when *he* found out that I was denying him, he'd looked so depressed. I couldn't stand seeing that beautiful man look so sad.

As I approached Albert's office, the person standing beside the door noticed me and announced my arrival. I was immediately led into the room.

When I first started coming by, I'd had to tell the guard at the door why I had come before he announced my arrival, but lately I was getting the VIP treatment. That seemed a little much, but no one said anything, so I tried to shrug it off. If I was doing anything weird, I hoped someone would say something.

"Hello," I said as I came in.

Albert greeted me with a dazzling smile. "What brings you here today?"

I lifted the basket hanging off my arm. "Aira and I did some baking today, so I brought you goodies."

"It's been a while since you last baked. You have my thanks." Albert accepted the basket with a pleased smile and handed it to the servant in the room.

The servant took the basket with practiced grace and walked out. He had presumably left to go fetch us some tea. How did I know that? Because that was what happened every time I brought baked goods to Albert.

"You'll have some with me, won't you?" Albert asked.

"Of course, if you'd like me to join you."

What did I tell you?

Albert invited me to sit on the sofa, so I did. A few moments later, the servant returned, pushing a cart. I smelled the delicate scent of tea from the teapot sitting on it.

"So, you made pound cake and cookies today?"

"Yup. I used the basic recipe, but hopefully it's not too sugary for your taste."

"That's quite all right. I can't wait to try them."

The servant filled the teacups and then placed them on the table alongside plates topped with cookies and slices of pound cake. Normally, I brought Albert specially made confections that were less sweet, but today I had brought him the same thing everyone else got. I didn't think it would go terribly, but I still worried that he might be less than pleased—hence my warning. But Albert didn't seem to share my caution as he took a bite of the pound cake.

My heart raced as I watched him chew. I was on tenterhooks, waiting to hear his opinion. Did he like it?

"It's delicious," he said with a smile.

A wave of relief washed over me, and I at last picked up my own plate.

"You made these with Aira?"

"The very one. I promised I'd bake with her a while ago."

"I see."

"That's why we stuck to the basic recipe. It's sweeter than what I usually make for you."

"Well then, that explains it. But don't worry, I find this level perfectly good."

"Oh, whew." I grinned, reassured.

I still thought it'd be nicer to make him a less sugary loaf of his own the next time I baked. I asked him if he would prefer that, just in case. He paused before nodding apologetically. I'd had a feeling!

"Sorry to make you go out of your way for me like that," he apologized.

"It's all right. I'd prefer to know your preferences so I can make things to your taste."

"Thanks. But I'd rather not be on the receiving end all the time," he murmured restlessly as he put a hand on his chin.

Uh-oh. Don't we have this conversation every time?

He asked me the question I knew was coming. "Is there anything you'd like to have?"

"Not really. Just seeing you enjoy my cooking is enough."

I was glad he'd at least asked me this time. The first time around, the conversation had gone something like:

"Dresses with narrow silhouettes have become fashionable. Would you like a new dress?"

"Oh, no, I couldn't possibly accept something so expensive in return for something as insignificant as cookies."

I turned Albert down every time, just like I had on the first, but he still hadn't given up. At first, he'd only asked about dresses, like what kind of designs I liked and such. After he exhausted that avenue, he'd moved on to asking me about accessories.

To be fair, there were an endless number of different kinds of accessories out there, so a lot of them would've been cheaper than a dress. However, I had a feeling that if

I agreed to anything, Albert would go and buy a version of that thing that was even more expensive than a ball gown. So, I didn't. I turned him down again that day, but somewhat unusually, he kept at it.

"I know you don't want anything, but..." Albert trailed off and furrowed his brow.

But he wants to give me a dress anyway? Or more like, he just wants to give me something—anything? Is that what he's about to say? Hoo boy, I hated the feeling that I was taking advantage of his generosity. I still gave him an inquisitive look and urged him to continue.

"I don't mind if it's something practical you'd wear any day," Albert said suddenly while averting his eyes. "I would just like to see you wearing something I picked out."

"Something practical?" I asked, just to make sure I had heard him correctly.

"Yeah." He looked back at me pleadingly, searching for an answer. He reminded me of an abandoned puppy. My resolve was shaken.

What should I do? It's okay to accept something practical, right?

"Do you like the color blue?" he asked.

"Blue?"

"Well, yes, I thought cloth in a light shade of blue would look nice on you."

That didn't really narrow it down. Which light shade was he thinking of? There was aqua, sky-blue, forget-me-not blue... White-violet too. Any of those hues could be likened to the color of Albert's eyes.

Which means that... My heart skipped a beat as I remembered a certain Salutanian custom. *No, wait. Calm down now. He still hasn't said that's what he intends to give me.*

My cheeks began to glow as I lowered my gaze to my feet. "Uh, yes, I do like the color blue."

"You do?" He sounded quite pleased.

"Um. An accessory with a blue stone set in it would probably look nice with light-blue cloth too." I was so unnerved that I tried to change the topic, but the next thing out of my mouth just helped me dig my own grave. I probably wasn't being melodramatic either.

Why did I bring up accessories?! I mentally wailed at myself as if I were part of some comedy routine, but it was too late.

"Then perhaps a sapphire," Albert happily murmured.

Whoa, wait! Sapphires are really expensive. Augh, oh man! I gotta come up with something else to talk about... Oh, I know!

"What about you?" I asked.

"Hmm?"

"What colors do you usually wear?"

"Hmm, good question. I prefer darker colors."

"You do?" I asked. *All right! I managed to change the subject. I'm surprised he likes wearing dark colors, though. He seems like the type who'd look good wearing any shade.*

Then Albert asked, "What color do you think would look good on me?"

"H-huh? Hmm..." He looked at me expectantly, and for some reason the room grew hotter. *Wait, does he want me to say that out loud? From my own mouth? But that would be super embarrassing!*

My cheeks grew hotter than ever as I racked my brain trying to come up with a way to survive this encounter.

◆ ◆ ◆

"Huh? Are those Sei's cookies?"

Aira's heart skipped a beat at the sound of the voice addressing her.

She had just started taking a break with some of her colleagues, so it wasn't like she was doing anything bad. However, something in Grand Magus Yuri's tone put her on edge. Everyone in the room simultaneously turned to look in the direction of the grand magus's voice and saw that Magus Erhart was with him.

The dread in the pit of Aira's stomach only grew. It was, to say the least, painfully awkward to be eyed by her bosses while she was taking a break.

But Yuri wasn't wrong. Aira was indeed serving cookies Sei had made, along with tea.

"You can tell?" one mage asked in surprise.

"Mm-hmm. I can see Sei's magic emanating from them."

While it was common knowledge that Yuri could see traces of magical power, Aira was surprised to learn that he could detect it on objects as well.

"May I have one?" Yuri asked. "I'm ready for a break myself, and something sweet might just do the trick."

The fact that Yuri and Erhart had just arrived together meant that they had likely returned from a meeting at the palace.

"Uhhh." The mage who had spoken glanced at Aira, expression unsure.

Aira timidly offered the plate of cookies to Yuri. "Sure, go ahead."

Yuri selected a cookie between his thumb and index finger and popped it into his mouth. A smile spread across his face. "Mm. Divine."

Aira let out a sigh of relief.

Out of the corner of her eye, she noticed Erhart watching Yuri closely, so she quickly offered him a cookie as well, feeling regretful for not offering him one in the first place. However, she soon began to worry that she shouldn't have. Erhart was her boss and the second strongest mage in the Assembly. She didn't want to be disrespectful.

However, contrary to Aira's fears, Erhart stretched his long fingers toward the cookies. As he ate, his expression remained utterly unchanged, but he nodded ever so slightly.

I'm guessing he liked it? Aira thought.

"Did you make some of these too, Aira?" Yuri asked.

"Huh?"

"I see that some of them have traces of your powers as well."

"Oh. Yes, that's right." Aira grew a bit flustered when this was pointed out.

Yuri picked another cookie, holding it high overhead as he voiced his admiration.

The other mages on break looked at Aira with a bit of surprise. Most of them were from noble families and had assumed that, like the majority of noble ladies, Aira couldn't cook.

"You know how to bake cookies, then?" Yuri asked.

"Yes. Just simple ones, though."

"Would you consider baking more later? You like sweet snacks and desserts, don't you?"

"Uh..." Aira's eyebrows knit at the suggestion. She

wouldn't have minded baking more, but she had no place to do so. There was a kitchen at Sei's Research Institute of Medicinal Flora but no such facility at the Assembly. She could ask Sei to let her borrow the kitchen, but she couldn't barge in all the time. As such, Aira was unsure of how to respond.

"Don't ask her to do something she can't," Erhart said.

Yuri pouted. "Why can't she, though?"

"Just go buy some, if you want them so badly."

"But the ones they sell at the market are too sweet."

Everyone glanced about, searching for an escape from this banter between their superiors.

"Besides, where would she even bake them?" Erhart continued. Though unaware of Aira's reason for hesitating, he had identified the main issue all on his own.

"Uh..."

"We have neither an oven nor a kitchen."

"Oh, that's right." Yuri's shoulders drooped. However, his frown brightened nigh instantaneously. "Then perhaps we should have them built here as well."

"What?"

"You'll be able to bake if we have the correct facilities, right?" Yuri looked at Aira eagerly.

Aira nodded nervously, inspiring a most powerful brow furrow on Erhart's part. It wasn't hard to guess why he was so troubled. Building a baking facility would incur quite a cost, and the Royal Magi Assembly had no such room in its budget.

"Do you have any idea how expensive it would be to build a kitchen?" Erhart demanded.

"Aw, are you saying we can't afford it?"

"Do you even have to ask?"

Yuri pouted again.

Meanwhile, Aira frowned thoughtfully. *It's true that making an oven that uses firewood would require a good deal of construction. But what if we just enchanted something, like Sei suggested?*

"Um, excuse me?" All eyes focused on Aira. Despite her anxiety, she managed to tell them about her conversation with Sei.

At present, the most an item enchanted with Fire Magic could do was heat a bit of water, but could they devise something with a bit more firepower? If they could, then maybe they could even create an enchanted oven. Aira had no idea whether it would cost more to construct a kitchen or to create such an enchantment, but she offered the idea anyway.

Erhart furrowed his brows again, as expected, but Yuri was dearly intrigued, no doubt because this was an opportunity to experiment with magic.

In the end, after Erhart worked out the cost of both ventures, they didn't get his permission. However, not much later, Yuri used his own funds to develop an enchanted oven. Of course he had been able to make it happen, what with his high level in Fire Magic and access to the abundant coffers of his adoptive family.

The Assembly couldn't put the oven on the market due to its exorbitant cost, but Yuri wore an incredibly satisfied look when he finished it. Of note, the two individuals he had interrogated nonstop about the inner workings of electric ovens in Japan were, by the end of it, exhausted.

It went without saying that the very first enchanted oven was installed in the Royal Magi Assembly barracks.

The Saint's Magic Power is Omnipotent

Bonus Story 2

"WELL, WHAT DO YOU THINK?" I asked a knight after he was done eating.

"It was delicious!"

Hm. Not the answer I'd been hoping for. I chuckled half-heartedly.

"That's not what she meant," a second knight told the first.

The first knight scratched his head and laughed sheepishly.

The dining hall at the Research Institute of Medicinal Flora was stuffed with people and lively for it. Normally, it was just me and my colleagues, but that day, the Knights of the Third Order had come to help me with some experiments.

By experiments, I meant specifically some tests I was running on spelt, a type of wheat I had found in Klausner's Domain. While there, I had discovered that food made with spelt increased HP recovery. However, I didn't yet know the mechanism; did it actively heal the body, or did it shorten the standard interval of HP recovery, or what? These experiments would help me sort that out.

I probably could have investigated spelt using my colleagues as my research subjects, but as spelt impacted HP recovery, I really wanted to use the knights. They were highly sensitive to tiny changes in their HP, seeing as their HP was depleted on the regular. Thus, I asked them to participate.

At least, that was what I told myself. The fact was that I was well aware that the knights really, *really* wanted to eat my pasta again.

"Take a look at your stats," the second knight told his friend. "We're here because we're supposed to be helping with her experiments."

"Yeah, come on," a third teased.

I nodded. "Yes, please let me know every time you recover some HP."

"Will do!"

"Got it!"

Enthusiastic as always.

Now that the knights were done eating, the next step was to check their stats. The knights opened their stats windows and focused on their HP count. Every time one of them reported a change, the researcher assigned to their table recorded it.

Those records were the last step of the experiment, so I headed over to a table in the corner of the dining hall to eat my own meal. I hadn't eaten lunch yet because I had been leading everyone else thus far. Two men were waiting for me there.

"Thanks for the hard work," said Johan.

"Yes, thank you," said Albert.

I had been planning to eat on my own, but the two of them had waited for me to eat. They thanked me for the meal as I sat. I let out a sigh of exhaustion as a chef brought over some pasta for us.

"My apologies. So many of my knights were begging to try it again," Albert said.

"That's all right. In fact, it's better to have lots of people participate. That means we'll have a much easier time pinning down the effect."

"It must have been hard to cook all of this though, right?"

I laughed to brush off his question. I was sure he'd work himself into a tizzy if I told him the truth. He seemed to catch on anyway, and he frowned.

Sorry... I can't say it was easy.

It had taken a ton of work to prep everything for the study. When I'd asked for volunteers, practically every single knight in the Order had raised his hand. Pasta was pretty popular in the Third Order, especially because those of them who hadn't accompanied me to Klausner's Domain had heard of its deliciousness from the knights who had.

Of course, the knights weren't the only ones eager to try new food. Everyone at the institute was hankering for a taste as well, starting with Johan.

As a result, I had been incredibly busy getting everything together. First, I'd had to teach the institute's chefs how to cook the pasta. Second, I'd had to design the study. I'd worked hard during the actual pasta-making part too—though I'd only watched during that last part. I hadn't wanted my fifty percent bonus curse messing things up. So perhaps I'd had it easy, in the end. The chefs were the ones who'd really had it rough.

Maybe I'll make dessert after. We bought so much spelt for this study that I could definitely make crepes too. Those are pretty easy.

"You were right, Al. Even though it's seasoned with nothing but herbs, this is delectable." Johan had clearly heard about Albert's prior pasta experience.

"See? What'd I tell you?" Albert enthused.

"Thank you," I said. "I do wonder if it would've been better not to add any of those for this study, though..."

"Oh, I'm sure there would've been a riot," said Albert.

Well, he's right. It would be weird to just eat salted noodles. Would they really riot, though? I reflexively glanced in the direction of some of the knights. *Surely Albert wouldn't let them get away with that, right?*

And then there was Johan. He nodded thoughtfully at Albert's observation. Come on, really?!

Once they finished, Johan joined the experiment. "*Stats*... I just can't tell."

"Maybe there's no change because you're at full HP?"

"That could be it."

We researchers were usually doing office work, so we rarely lost any HP. Sometimes our HP was affected when we got lightly poisoned, or that one time someone accidentally got hit with a laxative, but that didn't sound like something to experiment with. I had instantly shot the idea down when one of my colleagues brought it up.

I'd asked the knights to train before they came, so they weren't at full HP. However, as a result, they ate most of the pasta, which took me by surprise. I had underestimated their appetites.

I'll be sure to make even more for them next time.

Yup, this wasn't the only study I had in mind. I was planning to cook another dish with spelt in order to find out whether it was the *type* of food that induced this effect or if spelt itself yielded the effect in general.

Although we'd had to make a ton of food this time, our hard work paid off. We were able to determine that dishes made with spelt increased the rate at which HP was naturally recovered. Based on these findings, the officials at the palace began to reconsider the use of wheat. They intended to change the knights' field rations to spelt-based foodstuffs. It would be a great help to have this kind of effect on hand while they were out fighting monsters.

The dining hall at the institute kept using regular old wheat, though. We researchers just wouldn't benefit enough from the effect to make buying spelt worth it.

Spelt had been recognized as an exceptionally healthy food in my old world too. I was pretty interested in finding out just what benefits food could bring outside of the effects manifested by Cooking skills.

I contemplated this as I compiled my report on the results of the day's study. Johan noticed my distracted look and said, "Something the matter?"

"No, I was just thinking about something."

He glanced at my papers. "What about?"

"I'm wondering how good spelt is for the body outside of its skill-based applications. Like, could I use it in medicinal cooking?"

Johan touched his chin. "You never know. I imagine you could, but you'll only be able to confirm it one way or another with an experiment."

"True."

In the end, we decided that we needed to conduct more studies. This was no problem as research projects were the heart and soul of the Research Institute of Medicinal Flora. However, we wouldn't make any major breakthroughs right away—sorting this out would take patient, persistent research.

I already had my hands full with tons of projects, so I didn't think I could add this one to my immediate workload. This new idea of mine would just have to sit on the back burner.

Having come to that conclusion, I went back to writing my report.

The Saint's
Magic Power is
Omnipotent

Bonus Story 3

As I was brewing potions at the institute, Jude came into the workroom. "Sei, you have a visitor."

"Okay, be right there!"

"He's waiting in the parlor."

"Thanks."

"Johan's with him."

"He is?"

Maybe it was an official from the palace then.

A month had passed since my return from Klausner's Domain. Over that month, from time to time, the palace had sent me on numerous expeditions to slay monsters. Or perhaps it was more accurate to say that they had been calling on me to purge black swamps. After all, every place they sent me to had one.

The Saint's primary occupation was killing monsters

and purging black swamps. However, I had something of a side job at the research institute. As I did very much have to keep going out on all these expeditions, I was reconciled to the fact that research wasn't my priority. The palace officials' frequent expedition-related visits brought that home every time they showed up. They did always make sure to clear everything with Johan, as he was my direct supervisor.

The visitor Jude had alerted me to was indeed an official from the palace. Presumably, he would be asking me to go out on an expedition again.

I wonder where I'm headed this time?

"Sorry to have kept you waiting," I said as I entered the room, where I found Johan and the official seated across from one another.

Normally, the official would've just given me a slight bow from the sofa, but today he stood up to bow formally.

Huh? What's going on?

I glanced Johan's way, and he only gave me a silent shrug. Welp. I returned the official's bow before I sat down next to Johan.

The official went on to explain the purpose of his visit. It was about monster slaying, just as I had expected. That had to mean they had found another black swamp. There sure were a lot of them in this poor, beleaguered kingdom.

"All right, you found another swamp. Where is it this time?"

"No, ah, as it turns out..." The official's eyes darted anxiously to the side. He was finding it difficult to give me an answer.

What's with him?

I looked at Johan for an explanation, but he shook his head. No clue there either. We exchanged frowns and tilted our heads in question. We turned to peer at the official.

The man at last gathered himself and inhaled. "My deepest apologies. As it turns out, we have not found a black swamp at this time."

"You mean you just need my help killing monsters?"

"Correct." The official nodded, but his gaze remained fixed on the table. And on top of that, he seemed slightly pale.

Well, if they hadn't found a swamp, then there had to be so many monsters that the situation was exceptionally dire. As I pondered this, the official reluctantly offered a more detailed explanation.

In brief, the situation was *not* dire. In fact, the domain I was headed to next was relatively peaceful compared to the other places I had visited. According to the palace's investigation, a handful of monsters appeared there, but they were so few that the palace wouldn't even have to send any knights to take care of them. Despite that, there was a reason why they were asking me to go.

Upon hearing that, my face went full Tibetan fox levels of unimpressed. Yeah... Someone wanted to flex their power.

"We truly regret asking you to go afield for such a trivial reason, especially as you are so terribly busy..." the official trailed off before resuming his explanation. Poor guy had the look of someone prostrating themselves.

The palace didn't like the idea of dispatching the Saint for anything other than an emergency—especially not in cases when the person calling for the Saint's assistance seemed to care less about the danger than personal influence. Up until now, they had managed to come up with various reasons to turn down the more frivolous requests for my aid. However, this time, the person requesting my presence had refused to give up.

Unfortunately, the palace couldn't just reject the guy. I suspected that meant this noble was of high station. Furthermore, I hadn't been called on to head out in the field lately. This noble had noticed the lull, and he'd pounced on the opportunity to press the palace into sending me to his domain. With no more viable excuses to turn him down—i.e., no more black swamps—the palace finally had to yield to his request.

The official grew wearier and wearier as he relayed this information; I could tell this had been a fearsome battle.

I sighed. There wasn't any real significance to the sound, but the official's complexion went from regular pale to ghostly white.

I'm sorry! I'm not annoyed with you*—it's this noble who's ticking me off.*

I glanced at Johan from the corner of my eye. He was frowning at the official with real pity.

I dropped my voice to ask Johan, "Does this sort of thing happen often?"

"What do you mean?"

"Um, people abusing their ability to call upon the power of the state?"

"Ah, yes, it does." Johan nodded with a tired chuckle.

Though we'd lowered our voices, the official was definitely able to hear everything. I mean, he was seated directly across from us. He shrank back even more.

Well, what should I do about this? If I said no, this hapless official—stuck between this noble, the palace, and me—was going to have a heck of a time dealing with the fallout. Therefore, if Johan okayed it, I was willing to go. That didn't mean this noble's attitude didn't stick in my craw. I hated the idea of giving in quickly to a guy like that.

These kinds of things happened back in Japan too, I thought resentfully.

Meanwhile, Johan asked the official where I would be going. He winced in sympathy when the official relayed the location. It turned out that this noble was notorious for abusing his power to get his way.

"What's the local specialty in that domain?" I asked.

"As in, a local delicacy?" the official asked.

"Basically. If I have to go, then I'd like to check it out."

If this noble was obsessed with his own power, he was absolutely going to come up with all sorts of reasons to drag me around and treat me to nice things in order to curry my favor. I'd only ever been on the opposite side of this equation in Japan, but in my opinion, the whole rigmarole was a pain no matter which side you were on.

But if I had to deal with it, then I needed *something* to look forward to. As such, I wanted to enjoy the local specialty. Everywhere I had been thus far had developed some kind of unique offering. What did this domain have?

The official's complexion improved slightly; I had, after all, just said something about this whole situation that sounded somewhat positive. "Probably pork."

"Do you mean like pigs?"

"Indeed. They have fertile fields where they're able to raise a large number of pigs."

His smile returned as he told me more about the domain. I supposed it made sense that a noble with a lot of sway would rule over a domain with abundantly fertile land. Their ability to raise so many pigs was proof of that—not only were the people able to eat, they were also able to feed their livestock.

I wonder if they have ham and sausage. I'm kinda looking forward to that.

"What's on your mind?" Johan asked.

I grinned at him. "I was wondering about what they might have made with all that pork."

A grin spread across Johan's face as well. "Ah, I see."

*Wait a minute—*I'm *smiling because I'm looking forward to being treated to food. What's* he *smiling about?*

Honestly, it wasn't too hard to figure out. If we found a way to directly obtain high-quality pork, then I could make new pork dishes at the institute.

We'd been looking at one another while chatting, but now we turned back to the official.

"If Sei asks my permission, I believe I'll give it," Johan said.

"Okay. Then I'd like to go," I said.

"Thank you!" The official was so enthusiastically grateful that he practically threw himself at my feet.

He gave us a few more details before leaving. On his

way out, I made the official take some pound cake back with him—it had been our snack for the day. I felt awful knowing he would have to keep dealing with this noble. The guy sounded like a royal pain. Hopefully the sweet snack would help the long-suffering official feel better. He did look tremendously pleased with his gift.

At the entrance to the forest, I got out of the carriage and stretched. As I lowered my arms, I heard footsteps behind me. I turned to find myself facing someone with golden hair that glinted in the sunlight.

"Tired?" he asked.

"Nope, I'm fine." I smiled at Albert, which brought a smile to his face as well.

It was finally the day to go kill some monsters in the new domain. It had sure taken a while to reach this point, though...

The domain that had so persistently requested my aid was in fact fairly peaceful, with few if any monsters troubling the people—just like we'd heard. And, just as I predicted, I had been wined and dined by the domain's lord from the moment we arrived at his castle. I had been told it would just be until we headed out on our expeditions. For some reason—who could guess why!—that had taken a whole week.

There definitely weren't enough monsters to warrant that much preparation. I'd had the knights look into it for me to double-check, just in case.

Although I had known this would happen, having nothing to do had made me all kinds of restless. Now, I had finally escaped the lord's attempts to detain me, and we had at last made it to the forest. However, there weren't that many monsters in the forest to begin with.

We'll just go on a few forays, clear out the monsters, and then head straight home to the capital. After all, there might be another black swamp waiting for us by the time we get back.

The knights accompanying me shared this sentiment, so we got to work as soon as possible. We split into teams and entered the forest.

"There really aren't any monsters," I said after nearly a half hour of walking. We hadn't run into a single one.

"Well, of course there aren't. You're here with us," the knight walking next to me joked.

At that, another knight quietly chuckled.

Normally we weren't so carefree on an expedition, but the lack of monsters had put us all at ease. Even Albert was laughing.

"By the way, did you make the pasta we had last night?" the knight asked.

"That I did."

"I had a feeling. It was incredible."

I had indeed made pasta for the knights the night before. Specifically, I had used eggs and bacon to make carbonara. Although this domain was known for its pork, they also raised cows and had plenty of fresh cream and cheese. They also raised a number of chickens for eggs. The bacon had been made by one of the chefs in the castle.

I had borrowed the local lord's kitchens to cook. Once before, I had made a pasta dish in Klausner's Domain, and when I told the local lord that I wanted to make a new kind of dish with a different kind of sauce, he had readily agreed to let me use the kitchens.

Naturally, I hadn't forgotten to treat the lord and his family too. As one would expect from someone who had used his power to summon the Saint to his lands, he had been quite pleased to be able to taste the Saint's home cooking. It was thanks to this gift that I had received enough ingredients to make pasta for the knights as well. All in all, a win-win situation. Kind of.

"Pork sure is tasty," I said.

"It really is."

"I wonder if we can get the good quality stuff in the capital." I wanted to try making all kinds of dishes, if I could manage it.

Albert's eyes sparkled when I mentioned this. To be fair, the other knights' eyes did too.

Please don't look at me like you're looking at prey!

I was immediately interrogated about what kind of meals I wanted to make with pork, so I ran through a few possibilities based on what ingredients were available at the institute. There was a lot more I could make if only I had key ingredients. However, this world wasn't as developed as the world I had come from, so it was hard to get everything you wanted whenever you wanted it.

Nevertheless, Albert's mind was entirely focused on the prospect of new kinds of food to try.

In the end, there were only a few monsters to defeat, even in the depths of the forest. After a few more similarly fruitless runs, we reported to the lord that we had concluded our expeditions and returned to the capital. The lord tried to keep us around, but he couldn't force us to stay. We had indulged him enough when I decided to turn up in the first place.

The night we returned to the capital, I spent the evening resting to recover from the long journey. The following day, I went to Johan's office to let him know of my return.

"I'm back."

"Welcome back."

I gave him a brief report on the series of non-events that had been our expeditions. He laughed, as was his way.

"I figured as much," he said. "Good job hanging in there."

"Thank you."

"So? Did you get to enjoy the local specialty?"

Ha—he remembered how excited I'd been when we first talked about this. Admittedly, that excitement hadn't waned.

"I did!"

I told him about the pork dishes I'd made at the castle. I'd mostly only made traditional dishes that already existed in the Kingdom of Salutania's repertoire, which meant that Johan was able to comment on some of them as I described them. He'd had a number of these things before.

"Anything new?" he pressed.

"Actually, I'm pretty sure, yeah. And all because they had such a variety of livestock."

"Oh? Don't tease—what did you make?"

"A type of pasta called carbonara. It has a sauce made from eggs and smoked pork."

"Smoked pork..." Johan frowned.

It was technically possible to get bacon in the capital, but it was pretty expensive.

"I got a rasher of it as a souvenir from the lord, so I should be able to make it a few times."

"Really?!"

I had actually received a lot of presents from the lord as thanks for taking care of his teeny-tiny monster problem. Naturally, I had received bacon as well, so at least making carbonara wouldn't be a problem.

Johan smiled in pure delight upon hearing this news. Suddenly, his expression became that of someone who'd been struck by a profound epiphany. He thought for a moment with a hand to his chin. Then he grinned.

I could tell from his face—he'd come up with something *devious*.

"What?" I asked.

"Nothing, nothing. I believe I just thought of a way to regularly procure pork for the institute."

Still wearing that mischievous smile, Johan wrote a letter on the spot, which he handed to the servant who was waiting on him. The letter was addressed to the palace official who had visited us not long ago.

I had a feeling that I knew what Johan was up to. I learned how right I was a month later, when that very same official once more turned up at the institute.

It turned out that Johan had asked the official to handle securing scheduled shipments of pork for us—all due to that certain dish. He even managed to get the domain to sell us the pork at a steep discount...as recompense for the Saint's rather pointless visit.

Let me tell you, we got that pork *cheap*. Jude, who was from a family of merchants, couldn't suppress his admiration. The official had brought his A-game to negotiations with that lord. He seemed quite satisfied by the outcome, as he wore a big smile on his face as he reported it to us.

Now that we had a reliable supply of pork, I could increase the number of dishes on the dining hall's rotating menu. I wanted to try my hand at making all sorts of new foods with the help of my chef brigade. As I waved the official off, I began to plan my first experiment.

Afterword

HELLO, this is Yuka Tachibana. Thank you so much for picking up Volume Five of *The Saint's Magic Power is Omnipotent*.

I've heard from those who have also published novels that reaching Volume Five is a big milestone. I am incredibly grateful to everyone who supported me along the way to reaching it. Thank you.

As always, thank you to my editor, W from Kadokawa Books, for making every effort to adjust the schedule for me. Also, thank you for being there to give me advice about the plot details. It was such a huge help.

Thank you to the rest of the staff too. After we adjusted things a bit, I fully intended to follow the schedule as planned, but unfortunately things didn't go as I hoped.

I sincerely apologize for that. Surely, surely next time I'll work hard enough to be on schedule.

So, did you enjoy reading Volume Five? There will be some spoilers from this point on, so if you haven't finished reading the main story yet, please do so first!

It's pretty common to model a fictional city on one that exists in real life. However, I guess I'm bad at expressing my impressions about things or something, because I wasn't able to depict the city with that acute sense of realism I wanted, and I often felt like I needed to be more diligent.

I did indeed base Morgenhaven on a real city. It's a place with lots of precipitous slopes and hills, and it's famous for its fog. In fact, it was pretty foggy when I personally visited this city. It's amazing how many water droplets there are in fog. It felt like my face was covered in them—so much so that, at first, I thought it was drizzling. I had been in fog up in the mountains once before, but I'd been in a car, so I had never actually been outside right in the middle of it. I would never have imagined that it felt like being in rain.

There are a lot of things that are quite interesting to actually experience yourself. I guess another example would be really hot weather, which I got to experience a year ago during a business trip to the Kansai area. It was 104 degrees Fahrenheit! I feel like there's a real difference in heat between 90 and 100. It was *so* hot... The reflected heat from the asphalt was so ridiculously hot that I imagined that it had to feel like being in a desert.

I'll definitely think back on that experience if I ever write about a city in a desert. But before I do that, I would actually like to try going to a desert. I do love to travel.

Speaking of temperature, it's so interesting how much it can vary in a single day. When traveling from north to south, you can experience quite a range in twenty-four hours. The greatest shift I've ever personally experienced was forty degrees. It was like experiencing summer and winter all in one day. It occurred to me that I could use that to describe the general size of a continent. In fact, there is already a novel that does that.

There isn't such a big change in temperature in a single day's journey when traveling by carriage in the Kingdom of Salutania, but I hope you'll be able to get a feel for how big the continent is based on the places Sei goes.

Yasuyuki Syuri-sensei was once more in charge of the illustrations for this volume. Thank you for providing such lovely illustrations again. Seeing your thoroughly on-point character designs makes me pump my fist every time.

The designs for both Oscar and Ceyran look exactly like I imagined them. Actually, Ceyran looks even more handsome than I had imagined. Syuri-sensei does such amazing work. Thank you so much. (And thank you for the muscles too.)

The manga version of the story seems to be doing well also. I'm incredibly grateful to everyone reading it—and to all of the staff involved, starting with Azuki Fuji-sensei. Thank you always.

I checked many different illustration drafts that were included with Volume Five's release. Thank you so much for drawing Sei in a camisole and with glasses. It was a lovely extra. I'm always unsure about whether to announce what the extras are and often end up not mentioning them, but when I saw that one, I wanted to let everyone everywhere know about it.

You can read the popular manga version of this story at ComicWalker, pixiv Comic, and Nico Nico Seiga.* Part of the series is available to read for free, so please check it out if you're interested.

By the time Volume Five is released, I wonder how much of the story will be out. I have a feeling that Sei is going to make a big mess of things again soon.

There's one more person I need to thank this time.

To tell the truth, I had a very difficult time coming up with the plot for this volume. Back when I was writing the manuscript for Volume Three, I had thought up an outline for Volume Five, but it was hard to come up with ideas. It was then that the Demon Lord came to give me some advice.

Oh, the Demon Lord is the nickname I gave to one of my friends. Normally he goes by Kanzaki Kurone. He's the author of *Demon Lord, Retry!* Thanks to his help, I figured out the direction of Volumes Five and Six. Thank you so much for your help then. And I'm sorry for not introducing a young boy (inside joke).

Lastly, thank you so much for reading up until this point. I'll work hard to make sure Volume Six is in your hands as soon as possible. I hope we'll see each other again soon.

* *Look for it in English, also from Seven Seas!*